HARLEQUIN®

KISS™

W9-AMT-788

THE SECRET WEDDING DRESS

Through gritted teeth, Paige muttered, "That's it. I hereby promise to throw myself upon the mercy of the next man who smiles at me. I need to get myself some man-time and fast. Deal? Deal."

"Hold the door," said a deep male voice.

He loomed into view—a stranger, his bulk blocking her view of the foyer entirely.

As she pressed herself deeper into the small lift, her eyes flickered over a well-worn chocolate-brown leather jacket, with dark hair curling over the wool-lined collar, over dark denim clinging tight to masses of muscle, down to huge scuffed boots. Big and brawny, he was, with dark shadowed eyes and stubble long past designer on a jaw that could have been cut from granite.

The raw and unadulterated impact of the man sent her stomach into free fall, and the color rushed into her skin with a whoosh she could practically hear. She had to swallow down the sudden absurd urge to growl.

Then a husky voice inside her head sent the stranger a silent plea: *smile.*

DEAR READER,

My favorite moments writing are the ones I don't see coming. Impulses of inspiration that spring up from nowhere, like perfect little bubbles of narrative gold I have to sweet-talk onto the page before they pop. This book was full of them.

The story sprang from an image that just popped into my head one day, so clear to me it was like I was watching it unfold on film—a woman, standing in a lift, waiting for the doors to close, her arm aching from holding up a wedding dress, when in walks the man of her dreams. What was the story behind the dress? I had to know! As for how she was going to handle meeting the most gorgeous man she'd ever met…wedding dress in hand? Forget about it!

When my muse then sent me big, bad, dark, gorgeous Gabe Hamilton, with a voice so deep and rich, like how the devil ought to sound if he hoped to be any good at tempting people to the dark side… Well, there was no going back from there.

I'm so excited that *The Secret Wedding Dress* is my first Harlequin KISS title. The authors of Harlequin KISS are fantastic, and they write exactly the kinds of books I love to read—fun, flirty, sexy and real, with just the right dash of fantasy to make the reads as delicious as can be.

For more about my books, swing by my website, www.allyblake.com.

Til then, happy reading!

Ally

THE SECRET WEDDING DRESS

ALLY BLAKE

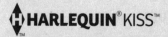

Recycling programs
for this product may
not exist in your area.

ISBN-13: 978-0-373-20708-4

THE SECRET WEDDING DRESS

www.Harlequin.com

ABOUT ALLY BLAKE

—

In her previous life, Australian author Ally Blake was at times a cheerleader, a maths tutor, a dental assistant and a shop assistant. In this life, Ally is a bestselling, multi-award-winning novelist who has been published in over twenty languages with more than two million books sold worldwide.

She married her gorgeous husband in Las Vegas—no Elvis in sight, though Tony Curtis did put in a special appearance—and now Ally and her family, including three rambunctious toddlers, share a property in the leafy western suburbs of Brisbane with kookaburras, cockatoos, rainbow lorikeets and the occasional creepy-crawly. When not writing, she makes coffees that never get drunk, eats too many M&Ms, attempts yoga, devours *The West Wing* reruns, reads every spare minute she can and barracks ardently for the Collingwood Magpies footy team.

You can find out more at her website, www.allyblake.com.

This and other titles by Ally Blake are available in ebook format. Check out Harlequin.com.

For Deb.
For your imagination, your encouragement,
your friendship. And for the bit about the lift.

THE SECRET
WEDDING DRESS

ONE

———

Paige Danforth didn't believe in happily ever afters.

So it was a testament to how awesome a friend she was that she stood freezing her tush off outside a dodgy-looking Collingwood warehouse in the grey half-light of a misty Melbourne winter's morning with her best friend Mae who was there to buy a wedding dress.

Wedding Dress Fire Sale! Over 1000 new and used dresses, up to 90% off! read the massive hot-pink banner flapping dejectedly against the cracked brown bricks of the old building. Paige wondered if any of the other women in the line, which by that stage snaked all the way around the corner of the block, saw the irony of the hype masking the depressing reality. By the manic gleams in their eyes they all bought into the fantasy, for sure. Each and every one of them convinced they were the ones for whom the love songs and sonnets rang true.

'The door moved,' Mae whispered, grabbing Paige's arm so tight she knew it would leave a mark.

Paige lifted her long hair out of the way so that she could loop her thick woollen scarf once more around her neck and stamped her boots against the pavement to get her sluggish blood moving. 'You're imagining things.'

'It jiggled. Like someone was unlocking it from the inside.' Mae's voluble declaration spread up and down the line like wildfire, and Paige was almost pushed over in the sudden surge of bodies.

'Relax!' Paige said, prying her friend's ever-tightening claw from her arm while glaring at the rabid-looking woman pressing close behind her. 'The doors will open when they open. You will find the dress of your dreams. If you can't find yourself a dress in a thousand, then clearly you're a failure as a woman.'

Mae stopped twitching to glare at her. 'I should rescind your Maid of Honour duties for that alone.'

'Would you?' Paige begged.

Mae laughed. Though it was short-lived. Soon she was jogging on the spot like a prize fighter seconds from entering the ring, her usually wild red hair pulled into a no-nonsense ponytail, her focus fixed, as it had been since the moment her boyfriend had proposed.

All of a sudden the flaky wooden doors were flung open with a flourish, the mixed scents of camphor and lavender spilling into the air with a sickly sweet rush.

A tired-looking woman in skinny jeans and a T-shirt the same hot pink as the sign above yelled, 'No haggling! No refunds! No returns! No sizes bar what's on the floor!' The words echoed down the narrow lane, and the line of women mushroomed towards the doors as if she'd announced Hugh Jackman would be giving free back rubs to the first hundred through the door.

Paige barely kept her feet as she pressed forward into the breach, and then grabbed Mae by the shoulders as she screeched to a sudden halt. Like Moses parting the Red Sea, waves of women poured around them.

'Holy moly,' Mae said.

'You're not wrong,' Paige muttered, as even she was impressed with what she saw.

Sweetheart necklines by the dozen, beaded corsets as far as the eye could see, sleeves so heavily ruched they made the eyes water. Designer dresses. Off the rack dresses. Second-hand dresses. Factory second dresses. All massively discounted. Every last one of them to be sold that day.

'Move!' Mae cried out as she came to and made a beeline for something that had caught her now frantic eye.

Paige quickly tucked herself in a corner in the shadow of the door. She waved her mobile phone in the air. 'I'll be over here if you need me!'

Mae's hand flapped briskly above the crowd of heads and then she was gone.

What followed was a lesson in anthropology. One woman near Paige who wore an immaculately tailored suit squealed like a teenager when she found the dress of her dreams. Another, in a twin-set, glasses, and tidy chignon, had a full-on temper tantrum, complete with stamping feet, when she discovered one didn't come in her size.

All for the sake of an overpriced dress they'd only wear once at a ceremony that forced people to make impossible promises to love, honour, and cherish for ever. In Paige's experience it was more like bicker, loathe, and cling on for dear life until there was nothing left but lost years and regret. Better to love, honour, and cherish yourself, Paige believed. For the chance to dress like a princess one time in your life the relentless search for love couldn't possibly be worth it.

The scents of hairspray and perfume mixed with the camphor and lavender and Paige soon had to breathe through her mouth. Her fingers curled tighter around her mobile, willing Mae to ring.

Mae. Her BFF. Her partner in crime. They'd had one another's backs for so long, since their parents had gone through simultaneous messy divorces and had left them both certain that happy ever after with some guy was an evil myth—one that had been perpetuated by florists and bakers and reception hall owners. Mae, who'd forgotten it all the moment she'd found Clint.

Paige swallowed. She deeply hoped Mae would be perfectly happy for ever and ever. She really did. But a hot spot of fear for her flared in her stomach every time she let herself think about it. So she decided to think about something else.

As brand manager for a luxury home-wares retailer, she was always on the lookout for locations in which to shoot catalogues, and, while the Collingwood warehouse was near decrepit, at a pinch the crumbling brickwork could be considered romantic.

Not that she wanted to shoot there any time soon. The next catalogue had to be shot on location in Brazil.

Period. Such a big expense for a single catalogue was as yet unheard of at Ménage à Moi, which was a boutique business, but Paige *knew* in her bones it would be worth it. Her proposal was so dazzling her boss had to say yes. And it was just the shake-up her life needed—

Paige shook her head. Brazil was the shake-up the *brand* needed. *She* was fine. Hunky-dory. Or she would be when she got the hell out of the building.

Breathing deep through her mouth, she closed one eye and imagined the massive windows draped in swathes of peacock-blue chiffon, the muted brickwork a total juxtaposition against the next season's dazzling, Rio-inspired, jewel-toned decor. Weak sunlight struck the glass which was in dire need of an industrial wash, made all the more obvious when compared with one incongruous clean spot that let through a single ray.

Dust mites danced in the sunbeam and Paige's eye naturally followed it all the way to a rack of wedding dresses, most of which boasted ridiculously excessive layers of skirt that would struggle to fit even the widest chapel aisle.

She made to glance away when something caught her eye. A glimpse of chiffon in dark champagne. The iridescent sheen of pearls. Impossibly intricate lacework. A train so diaphanous it was lost as someone walked by the rack, blocking out the ray of light.

Paige blinked. And again. But the dress was gone. And her heart skipped a beat.

She'd heard the expression a million times, only had never experienced it until that moment. Didn't realise it came complete with a tightening of her throat, a sudden lightness in her head, and the complete cessation of thought.

Then someone moved, the ray of light returned, and there it was. And then she was standing. Walking. At the rack, her hands went to the fabric as though possessed by some other-worldly force. The garment came to her from between the tight squeeze of dresses as easily as Arthur had released Excalibur from its stone prison.

As her eyes skimmed over the softly twisted straps, the deep V, a torso of lace draped in strings of ocean pearls that cinched into the most exquisite silhouette before disappearing into a skirt made of chiffon that moved as if it breathed, Paige's heart galloped like a brumby with a horse thief hot on its heels.

'Wow,' a voice said from behind her. 'That's so cute. Are you just looking or do you have dibs?'

Cute? That was the best word the woman could come up with for the sliver of perfection draped over Paige's shaking hands.

Paige didn't even turn around. She just shook her head as the words she'd never thought she'd hear herself say escaped her lips:

'This wedding dress is mine.'

'Paige!'

Paige looked up from her position back near the doors to find Mae literally skipping towards her.

'I've been trying to call you for twenty minutes!'

Paige's hand went to her phone in her pocket. She hadn't felt a thing. In fact, by the intensity of the light now pouring into the building, much of the morning had passed by in a blur.

Mae pointed madly at the heavy beige garment bag hooked over one crooked elbow. 'Success! I wanted you to see it but I couldn't get hold of you and this skinny brunette was eyeing it up like some starving hyena, so I stripped down to my bra and knickers and tried it on in the middle of the floor. And it's so freaking hot.'

Mae's eyes were now flickering to the fluorescent white garment bag with the hot-pink writing emblazoned across the front that was draped over Paige's thighs. 'Did you find a bridesmaid's dress?'

Paige swallowed hard and slowly shook her head. Then, unable to say the words, she waved a wobbly arm in the direction of the sea of white, ivory, and champagne frou-frou.

'Oh. For a catalogue shoot? You're doing a wedding theme?'

And there it was. The perfect out. The exorbitant dress was a work expense. That would even make it tax deductible and less taxing on her mortgage payments. But panic had clogged her throat shut tight.

Mae's eyebrows slowly slid skyward. Then after several long seconds, she burst out laughing. 'I thought I was the one who made bizarre shopping decisions when I wasn't getting any, but this takes the cake.'

Paige found her voice at last. 'What's *that* supposed to mean?'

Mae's spare hand went to her hip. 'Tell me quick, without having to think about it, when was the last time you went on a date?'

Paige opened her mouth to say when, and who, and

where, but again nothing came out. Because for the life of her she couldn't remember. It had been weeks. Maybe even months. Rather than worry that she hadn't even noticed she hadn't been on a date in an age, she clutched onto the hope that there might be a reasonable reason for her moment of shopping madness.

'You need to get yourself a man and soon.' Mae tucked her hand through the crook of Paige's arm and dragged her to her feet. 'But until then let's get out of here before the smell of spray-tan and desperation makes me pass out.'

Paige stood in the single lift of the Botany Apartments at New Quay at Docklands, staring blankly at the glossy white and black tiled lobby floor, the decadent black paisley papered walls, the striking silver sun-bursts framing every door, all lit by the diffused light of a half-dozen mother-of-pearl chandeliers as she waited for the doors to close.

Was Mae right? Had her wholly daft purchase been the result of a recent spate of accidental abstinence? Like a knee-jerk reaction in the opposite direction? Maybe. Because while she had no intention of following Mae's path down the aisle, she liked dating. Liked men just fine. She liked the way they smelt, the way their minds worked, the curl of heat when she was attracted. She liked men who could wear a suit. Men who paid for drinks and worked long hours as she did and weren't looking for anything more than good company. The kind of men downtown Melbourne was famous for.

So where had they all gone?

Or was it her fault? Had all the extra energy she'd put into the Brazilian catalogue proposal taken it out of her? Or was she bored with dating the same kind of guy all the time? Maybe she was emotionally sated by the *Gilmore girls* reruns on TV.

Groaning, she transferred the heavy white garment bag from one hand to the other, flexed her empty hand, and waited for the lift doors to close. And waited some more. It could take a while.

The lift had a personality all of its own, and as personalities went it was rotten to the core. It went up and it went down, but in a completely random fashion that had nothing to do with the floor she chose. Telling Sam the Super hadn't made a lick of difference. Neither had kicking it. Perhaps she should next try kicking Sam the Super.

Until then, all she could do was wait. And remind herself that a tetchy lift was a small price to pay for her little slice of heaven on the eighth floor. She'd grown up in a huge cluttered house filled with chintz and frilly curtains, and smelling of Mr Sheen and dried flowers and tension you could cut with a knife. And the first time she'd seen the sleek, open-plan opulence of the Botany Apartments she'd felt as if she could breathe fully for the first time in her life.

She closed her eyes and thought about the minimalist twenties decor in her apartment, the sliver of a view of the city, the two great-sized bedrooms—one for her, the other her home-office-slash-Mae's-room when Mae was too far gone after a big night out to make it home. Though it had been an age since Mae slept over. Not since around the time Clint proposed, in fact.

Paige shook her head as if shooing away a persistent fly. The point was the lift was a tiny inconvenience in the grand scheme of things. Except those times when she was carrying something that weighed the equivalent of a small car.

Okay. If datelessness had led to the *thing* currently giving her shoulder pain, then she needed to do something about it. And fast. Or who knew what she might do next? Buy a ring? Hire the Langham? Propose to herself in sky-writing?

As her spine began to crumple in on itself Paige muttered, 'I hereby promise to throw myself upon the mercy of the next man who smiles at me. He can buy me dinner first. Or I can buy him a coffee. Heck, I'll share a bottle of water from the third-floor dispenser. But I need to get some man time and fast.'

An absolute age later, when the lift doors *finally* began to close, she almost sobbed in relief. Until at the last second a row of fingers jammed into the gap.

'Hold the door,' said the deep male voice on the end of the long brown fingers.

No-o-o! Paige thought. Once those doors opened, the wait for the perverse damn lift to head skywards would start over, and she might never get the feeling back in her shoulders again.

'No?' the male voice asked with a low note of incredulity, and Paige blanched, realising she must have said it out loud. It seemed years of living on her own had made her a little too used to talking to herself.

Feeling only the slightest twinge of guilt, she jabbed at the 'close door' button. Repeatedly.

But the long brown male fingers had other ideas.

They prised that stubborn door open with what was a pretty impressive display of pure brute strength. And then he loomed into view, a stranger, a great big broad one, his bulk blocking her view of the foyer entirely. Head down, brow pinched into a frown, he stared intently at the shiny smartphone in his spare hand.

Something about him had Paige pressing herself deeper into the small lift. Something else entirely had her eyes flickering rapidly over a well-worn chocolate-brown leather jacket with thick dark hair curling over the wool-lined collar. Over soft denim, lovingly hugging masses of long hard muscle, the perfect lines broken only by a neat rectangular bulge where his wallet sat against his backside. Down to huge scuffed boots. *Huge.*

Any calm and soothing thoughts the view of mother-of-pearl chandeliers and silver sun-bursts had inspired were swept away by the raw and unadulterated impact of the man. The sweet curl of heat she'd been thinking about earlier rushed into Paige's stomach like a tidal wave and colour rushed into her skin with a whoosh she could practically hear.

Then, before she even had a chance to collect herself, a husky voice inside her head sent the stranger a silent plea: *Smile.*

Paige all but coughed on her own shock. *He* was not what she'd meant when she'd decided to get herself a man. A comfortable re-entry was just the ticket. Honestly, who needed such a breathtaking expanse of male shoulders, or such thick dark hair that looked as if no amount of product could completely ever tame it? Or fingers strong enough to open a lift door? As for the hint of hooded dark eyes she could make out in profile and stubble long past designer? That kind of intensity wasn't comfortable. It was overkill.

She was staring so hard at the man's lips—thinking that they were too ridiculously perfect to be hidden amongst all that rough stubble—there was no missing it when they twitched, as if they might be about to actually smile.

Oh, God, Paige thought as the man slid his phone into the inner pocket of his jacket. She'd been caught staring. And the pink warmth turned into a red hot inferno beneath her skin.

'Thanks for holding,' the stranger said in a voice that was deep and rich, like how the devil ought to sound if he hoped to be any good at tempting people to the dark side.

'My pleasure,' said Paige, eyes flickering up to his, which was why she didn't miss a millimetre of his eyebrow raise, reminding her he was perfectly aware of her attempt to sabotage his ride.

Quitting while she was behind, Paige shut her mouth and made room, plastering herself as far to one side of the small lift as possible. The sooner he got to wherever he was visiting, the better.

Naturally the lift was narrow, complementing the dinky design of the boutique apartment building, and the sizeable stranger seemed to fill every spare inch of space all by himself. Even the bits he didn't physically invade seemed to pulse with his energy. Every time he breathed in the hairs on Paige's arms stood on end.

'What floor?' he asked.

'Eighth,' she said, her voice gravelly as she waggled

a finger at the number-eight light that was lit up all hopefully.

The stranger ran a hand across the back of his neck and then the corner of his mouth lifted.

Paige held her breath while her hormones whooped up a series of cat-calls deep in her belly. But it wasn't a smile. Not officially. Even though it sure hinted at the kinds of eye crinkles that had a habit of turning her knees to water.

'Long flight,' he said, his deep voice rumbling through the floor of the lift and all the way up her legs. He lifted one ridiculously broad shoulder over which a leather satchel and a laptop bag hung. 'Not all here.'

Not all here? Any more of him and Paige would be one with the wall.

When the stranger leaned across to press the button to shut the doors Paige's skin tingled and tiny pinpricks of sweat tickled down her neck and spine. She breathed in and caught the scent of leather. Of spice. Of fresh chopped wood. Of sea air. Sweat that wasn't her own.

Outside it was the depth of winter, yet she yanked her scarf away from her neck and thought about ice cream and snowball fights to counteract the certainty that she was about to overheat. Yet something about him, something dark and dangerous dancing in his eyes, in the way her skin hadn't stopped thrumming from the moment she'd laid eyes on him, made her quite sure, no matter how many snowballs she imagined, it would never be enough.

He pulled back and grunted when the lift didn't move, and finally Paige's brain caught up with her hormones. 'Oh, no, no, no,' she said, 'there's really no need to press that button. Or any button. This lift is completely contrary. It rises and falls as it pleases, with no care at all for—'

With its usual impeccably bad timing, the lift doors slid neatly closed, the box juddered and after an infinitesimal drop it took off. Paige glared in disbelief at the indicator light above the doors, which lit up in actual sequential order as it rose smoothly towards the sky.

Rotten, stinking, little—

'You were saying?' the stranger said.

Paige's eyes cut to his to find humour now well and truly lighting them, creating fiery glints in the dark depths. As if he was about to smile at any second.

Okay, so that deal she'd made earlier to herself, it had been more like a set of guidelines than a promise. What if some pimply sixteen-year-old on a skateboard had smiled first? Or if it had been the guy with the scraggly beard and the rat on his shoulder who walked up and down the Docklands promenade yelling at seagulls? Clearly her deal needed tweaking before it went into *official* effect.

She lifted a shoulder, trying for nonchalance as she said, 'This lift has it in for me, clearly. While you, on the other hand, have the touch. Want a job as a lift operator? I'd pay you myself.'

The stranger's expression warmed. No, *burned*. As if the temperature of the glint in his eye had turned up a notch.

'Thanks for the offer,' he said, 'but I'm set.'

And had he moved closer? Or merely shifted his weight? Either way the lift suddenly felt smaller. The hairs on the back of Paige's neck now joining the party as they stood to attention.

'Oh, well. It was worth a shot.'

When the beautiful bow of his top lip began to soften sideways, Paige smartly turned to watch the display as the floor numbers rolled over all too slowly.

'You live in the building?' the stranger asked.

Paige nodded, biting her lip so as not to shiver as that dark velvety voice rolled over her skin in delicious waves.

'That explains your...relationship with the lift.'

Before she could help herself, her eyes slid back to the stranger, fully expecting to find him looking at her as if she might wig out at any second, as Sam the Super always did when she made a complaint. But the stranger's gaze was making its way over her hair, the curve of her neck, pausing a beat on her mouth, before coming back to connect, hard, with her eyes.

Her next breath in was long and deep, and once again filled with the scents of spice, and all things deeply masculine. Maybe she wasn't hallucinating. Perhaps he was a fighter pilot/lumberjack/yachtsman by trade. It could happen.

'It started out slow,' she said, sounding as if she'd run a mile in a minute flat, 'a missed floor here and there. But now it's all the time. I keep pressing the button knowing it'll make not a lick of difference, as I refuse to stop hoping it will one day simply start acting like a normal lift. While it won't stop refusing to be one.'

'Such friction,' he said, laughter lighting his eyes. 'A clash of equal and opposite wills. Like something out of a Doris Day and Rock Hudson flick.' He glanced at the computerised electronic display of her nemesis. 'With a sci-fi bent.'

Completely unexpectedly, Paige laughed out loud, the sound bouncing off the walls of the tiny lift. And this time when her eyes snagged back on his they stuck. Such dark eyes he had, drawing her in so deep, so fast, she wouldn't have noticed if the lift started humming *Pillow Talk*.

The only explanation she had for her reaction to him was her dating drought. He was so against type. She normally gravitated to men who were so clean cut they were practically transparent. Men who'd not have blinked had she slipped them a dating contract: three nights a week, split checks, no idealistic promises.

Whereas this man was so dark, enigmatic, and diabolically hot every nerve in her body was fighting against every other nerve. His big body that made her palms itch, and his scent that made her want to lean in and bury her face in his neck. 'Getting back on the horse' with a man like that would be akin to falling off a Shetland pony at the fair and getting back on a stallion jostling at the starting gate of the Melbourne Cup.

And yet… She wasn't after a dating contract. She needed a springboard from which to leap back into the dating world. And there *he* stood, beautiful, sexy, and glinting at her like nobody's business.

She stuck out a hand. 'Paige Danforth. Eighth floor.'

'Gabe Hamilton. Twelfth.'

'The penthouse?' she blurted before her tongue could catch up with her brain. That was how addled she was; she hadn't even noticed which floor he'd pressed.

The penthouse had been empty since the day she'd moved in. Meaning... 'You're *not* visiting.'

'Not.' How the guy managed to make one word evoke so much she had no idea, but he evoked plenty. The fact that he would be sleeping a mere four floors above her being the meat of it.

'Renting?' she asked, and his eye crinkles deepened, making her wonder what she'd evoked without meaning to.

'Mine,' he drawled.

Paige nodded sagely, as if they were still talking real estate, not in non-verbal pre-negotiations for something far less dry. 'I hadn't heard it had been sold.'

'It hasn't. I've been away. And now I'm back.' For how long he didn't say, but the glint sizzling in his dark eyes and making her feel as if steam were rising from her clothes told her he believed it was long enough.

The lift dinged, as lifts were wont to do—normal lifts, lifts that weren't demonically possessed—right as she was gaining momentum to do something rash. Rash but necessary.

And then the doors opened.

'Of course,' Paige muttered as she recognised her own floor by the dotted silver wallpaper, a Ménage à Moi staple. What could she do but step out?

The back of her hand brushed Gabe's wrist as she shucked past. The lightest possible touch of skin on skin. When little waves of his energy continued crackling through her as she stepped out into the hall, Paige turned back. It was on the tip of her tongue to ask him in for coffee. Or offer to show him the sights of

Melbourne. Or any other number of euphemisms for breaking her dating drought.

Then he stifled a yawn.

Like the dawning of the sun it occurred to her that the glint in his eyes had probably been the effect of jet lag the entire time, not some kind of extraordinary instant mutual chemistry between herself and the vision of absolute masculine gorgeousness gracing the lift before her.

If her complexion had been tomato-esque earlier, she'd bet right about then she resembled a fire engine.

Please, she silently begged the lift as they stood facing one another, *close now. Just this once. Close.*

And it did. The two great silver doors slid serenely towards one another, Gabe's dark figure growing darker by the second. Until his hand curled around the edge of one door, stopping it in its tracks. Mere mechanics no match for his might.

'I'll see you 'round, Paige Danforth, eighth floor,' Gabe said, before his fingers slid back away.

Then, as the doors came to a close, he smiled. A dark smile, a dangerous smile, a smile ripe with implications. A smile that sent the dancing hormones inside her belly into instant spontaneous combustion.

Then he was gone.

Paige stood in the elegant hallway, breathing through her nose, feeling as if that smile would be imbedded upon her retinas, and messing with her ability to walk in a straight line, for a long, long time.

The gentle whump of the lift moving up inside the lift shaft brought her from her reverie and she blinked at the two halves of her reflection looking back at her in the spotless silver doors.

Or more specifically at the huge, great, hulking, fluorescent-white garment bag hanging from her right hand. The one she'd completely forgotten about even while her right hand now felt as if it would never feel the same again.

The one with the hot-pink words 'Wedding Dress Fire Sale!' glaring back at her in reverse.

TWO

—

'I'll be damned,' said Gabe to the dark wood panelling on the inside of the lift doors as he rubbed at the back of one hand with his thumb where the heat from the touch of his new neighbour's skin still registered.

During the endless trudge through Customs, the drive from the airport with its view over Melbourne's damp grey cityscape, then with the winter wind blowing in off Port Phillip Bay and leaching through his clothes to his very bones as he'd waited for the cabbie's credit card machine to work, Gabe had struggled to find one thing about Melbourne that had a hope in hell of inducing him to stay a minute longer than absolutely necessary.

Then fate had slanted him a sly wink in the form of a neighbour with wintry blue eyes, legs that went on for ever, and blonde tousled waves cool enough to bring Hitchcock himself back to life. Hell, the woman even had the restive spark in her eye of a classic Hitchcock blonde; fair warning to any men who dared enter it would be at their own peril.

Not that he needed any such warning. Three seconds after he signed whatever his business partner, Nate, wanted him to sign he'd be on the kerb whistling for a cab to get him back to the airport. Not even the kick of chemistry that had turned the small space of the lift into a travelling hothouse would change that.

Gabe rehitched his bags, then shoved his hands into the deep pockets of his jacket, closed his eyes and leant back into the corner of the lift. As the memory of where he was, and why he'd left in the first place, pressed against the corners of his mind he shook it off. And, merely because it was better than the alternative, he let his thoughts run to the cool blonde instead.

About the way she'd nibbled at her full lower lip, as if it tasted so good she couldn't help herself. And the scent of her that had filled the small space, sweet and sharp and delicious, making his gut tighten like a man who hadn't eaten in a week. As for the way she'd looked at him as if he was some great inconvenience one moment, and the next as if she wanted nothing more than to eat him up with a spoon...?

'Wow,' he shot out, eyes flying open, hands gripping the railing that ran hip high along the back of the lift, feet spread wider to combat the sudden sense that his centre of gravity had shifted. The lift had rocked. Hadn't it? Try as he might he felt nothing but the gentle sway as it rose through the shaft.

Jet lag, he thought. *Or vertigo.* He sniffed out a laugh. He had Hitchcock on the brain. The guy was no dummy and was also clearly terrified of cool blondes.

Did one thing inform the other? No doubt. If a woman looked like trouble, chances were she'd be trouble. And Gabe was a straight-up guy who preferred his pleasures the same.

He pulled himself to standing and ran both hands over his face. He needed sleep. Clearly. He imagined his custom-built king-sized bed which a week earlier he'd had shipped back from South America. The deal there was done anyway, and he'd ship it out again the second the next investment opportunity grabbed him. He imagined falling face down in the thing and sleeping for twelve hours straight.

For some, home was bricks and mortar. For others it was family. For Gabe it was where the work was. And wherever in the world he got wind of an exceptional business idea in need of someone with the guts and means to invest, that was where he sent his bed. And his pillow—flattened to the point he probably didn't even need the thing. And his mattress with the man-shaped dint right smack bang in the middle that fitted his spreadeagled body to perfection.

Moments before he fell asleep on his feet the lift deposited him neatly at his floor. Exactly as it was made to do.

Gabe yawned till his ears popped, fumbled for the keys to the apartment he'd never seen. The apartment he'd bought to shut Nate up, when Nate had maintained he needed a place in Melbourne considering the company they jointly owned was based there.

He stood in the open doorway. Compared with the bare-bones hotel room that had been home the past few months it was gargantuan, taking up the entire top floor of the building. And yet somehow claustro-phobic with its dark colour palette and the huge grey windows along one wall that matched the drizzly grey world outside them.

'Well, Gabe,' he said to his blurry reflection, 'you're certainly not in Rio any more.'

He slid the carry-on and laptop bags from his shoulder onto the only piece of furniture in the whole room, a long L-shaped black lounge that cut the space in half. Only to be met with a loud 'Arghuraguragh!'

Jet lag and/or vertigo gone in an instant, Gabe spun on his heel, fists raised, heart thundering in his chest, to find a man reposing on his couch.

'Nate,' Gabe said, bent at the waist, hands on his knees as he dragged his breath back to normal. 'You scared me half to death.'

Gabe's best mate and business partner sat up, his hair sticking up at the side of his head. 'Making sure you got here in one piece.'

'Making sure I arrived at all, more like.' Gabe stood, cricked his back. 'Tell me you went one better and filled my fridge.'

'Sorry. Did get doughnuts though. They're on the bench.'

Gabe glanced at the familiar white box as he passed it on the way to the silver monolith of a fridge, opening it to find it was empty bar the maker's instructions. A frisson of disquiet skittered down his spine. If that wasn't ready...

He strode across the gargantuan space towards the great double doors he could only assume led to the bedroom, whipped them open to find—

No bed.

Swearing beneath his breath, Gabe ran his hand up and down the back of his neck so fast he felt sparks.

Nate's hand landed upon his shoulder a half-second before his laughter. 'Your couch looks a treat but it's not in the least bit comfortable.'

'You didn't seem to mind a moment ago,' Gabe growled.

'I can power-nap anywhere. It's a gift born of chronic insomnia.'

Gabe slowly and deliberately shut the bedroom doors, unable to even look at the space where his bed ought to be.

'Hotel?'

'The thought of going back out into that cold is making my teeth ache.'

'I'd offer my couch, but it's my decorator's cruel joke. God-awful leather thing with buttons all over it.'

'Thanks, but I'd be afraid I'd catch something.'

Nate grinned and backed away. 'I have seen with my own two eyes that you're here, so my work is done. Catch you at the office Monday. Remember where it is?'

Gabe's answer was a flat stare. He was lucky—or unlucky more like—to end up in Melbourne once every two or three years, but he knew where his paychecks came from.

Nate clicked his fingers as he wavered at the front door. 'Almost forgot. Need to make a right hullabaloo now you're back. Housewarming party Friday night.'

Gabe shook his head. He'd be long gone by Friday. Wouldn't he?

'Too late,' said Nate. 'Already in motion. Alex and

some of the old uni gang are coming. A few clients. Some fine women I met walking the promenade just now—'

'Nate—'

'Hey, consider yourself lucky. I'm so giddy you're here I contemplated dropping flyers from a plane.'

And then Nate was gone. Leaving Gabe in his dark, cavernous, cold, empty apartment. Alone. The grey mist of Port Phillip Bay closing in on his wall of windows like a swarm of bad memories, pretty much summing up how he felt about the possibility that he might still be there in a week's time.

Before he turned into a human icicle, Gabe tracked down the remote for the air-con and cranked it up as hot as it would go.

He found some bed linen in a closet, then, back in his bedroom doorway, looked glumly at the empty space where his bed ought to be. He stripped down to his smalls and made a pile with blankets and a too big pillow and lay down on the floor, and the second he closed his eyes fatigue dragged him into instant sleep.

And he dreamt.

Of a cool feminine hand stroking the hair at the back of his neck, a hot red convertible rumbling beneath his thighs as he eased it masterfully around the precarious roads of a cliff face somewhere in the south of France. When the car pulled into a lookout, the cool owner of the cool hand slid her cool blonde self onto his lap, her sweet sharp scent hitting the back of his mouth a half-second before her tongue followed. Gabe's dream self thought, *Hitchcock, eat your heart out.*

* * *

That night at The Brasserie—one of a string of crowded restaurants lining the New Quay Promenade—when Mae told her fiancé, Clint, about Paige's little purchase, he choked on his food. Literally. A waiter had to give him the Heimlich. They made quite a stir, ending up with the entire restaurant cheering and Paige hunching over her potato wedges and hiding her face behind both hands.

Clint recovered remarkably to ask, 'So what happened between us pouring you into a cab after drinks last night and this morning to have cured you of your no-marriage-for-Paige-ever stance? Cabbie give you the ride of your life?'

Paige dropped her fingers to give Clint a blank stare. Grinning, he put his hands up in surrender before smartly returning to checking the footy scores on his phone.

She didn't bother telling him there had not been any curing her doubt as to the existence of happily ever afters. But she neglected to say that there had been one ride she couldn't seem to wipe from her mind. A ride in a lift with some kind of tall, dark and handsome inducement that got a girl to thinking about all sorts of things she wouldn't admit out loud without the assistance of too many cocktails.

She dropped her hands to her belly where she could still feel the hum of his deep voice.

As she'd done a dozen times through the day, she brought her thoughts back to the fluoro white bag covered in hot-pink writing currently hanging over the back of her dining chair.

The fact that Gabe Hamilton had got his flirt on while she was carrying a wedding dress made him indiscriminate at best. And the kind of man she wouldn't touch with a ten-foot pole. Fidelity meant a great deal to Paige. She'd worked for the same company since uni. Had the same best friend since primary school. She'd drive twenty minutes to get her favourite Thai takeaway. She'd watched her own mum crumble before her very eyes as her father confirmed his own disloyalty again and again and again.

'Humona humona,' Mae murmured, or something along those lines, dragging Paige back to the present. 'Move over, Captain Jack, there's a new pirate in town.'

Clint glanced up. Whatever he saw was clearly of little interest as he saw his chance to sneak a pork rib from Mae's plate then went back to his phone.

Paige gave into curiosity and turned to look over her shoulder, her heart missing a beat, *again*, when she found Mr Tall, Dark and Handsome himself warming his large hands by the open fire in the centre of the room, his dark hair curling slightly over the collar of his bulky jacket, feet shoulder width apart.

'Look how he's standing,' Mae said, her voice a growl.

As if used to keeping himself upright in stormy seas, Paige thought.

Mae had other ideas. 'Like he needs all that extra room for his package.'

'Mae!'

Mae shrugged. 'Don't look at me. Not when you could be looking at him.'

Paige tried not to look, she really did. But while her

head knew it was best to forget about him, her hormones apparently had fuzzier principles. She looked in time to see him push a flap of his leather jacket aside and glide his phone from an inside pocket, revealing a broad expanse of chest covered by a faded T-shirt. Paige wasn't sure which move had her salivating more—the brief flash of toned brown male belly as his T had lifted, or the rhythmic slide of his thumb over the screen of his phone.

And then he turned, his dark eyes scouring the large space.

'Get down!' Paige spun around and hunkered down in her seat until she was half under the table. It was only when she realised neither of her friends had said anything that she glanced up to find them both watching her with their mouths hanging open.

'Whatcha doin' down there?' Mae asked.

Paige slowly pulled herself upright. Then, wishing she had eyes in the back of her head, she muttered, 'I know him.'

'Him? Oh, *him*. Who *is* he?'

'Gabe Hamilton. He's moved in upstairs. We met in the lift this morning.'

'Annnnndddd?' Mae said, by that stage bouncing on her chair.

'Sit still. You're getting all excited for nothing. I tried to shut the door on his fingers. He suggested the lift and I were trapped in a passive-aggressive romantic entanglement. It was all very...awkward.'

Mae kept grinning, and Paige realised she was squirming on her seat.

She threw her hands in the air. 'Okay, fine, so he's

gorgeous. And smells like he's come from building his own log cabin. And there might have been a little flirting.' When Mae began to clap, Paige raised a hand to cut her off. 'Oh no. That's not the best part. This all happened right after you dropped me off. While. I. Was. Carrying. The. Wedding. Dress.'

'But didn't you explain—?'

'How exactly? *So, sexy stranger, see this brand new wedding dress I'm clutching? Ignore it. Means nothing. I'm free and clear and all yours if ya want me.*'

'That'd work for me,' Clint said, nodding sagely.

Mae smacked him across the chest. He grinned and went back to pretending he wasn't listening.

'I blame you, and your man-drought theory,' Paige said. 'I would have been hard pressed not to flutter my eyelashes at anyone at that point.'

'Like if Sam the Super had turned up she would have wanted to ravage him in the lift?' Mae muttered, shaking her head as if Paige had gone loco.

Paige couldn't stop feeling as if the world was tilting beneath her chair. Mae, of all people, should have understood her need for absolutes. The old Mae would, what with her own father's inability to be faithful. This new Mae, the engaged Mae, was too blinded by her own romance to see straight.

Paige fought the desire to shake some sense into her friend. Instead she reached for her cocktail, gulping down a mouthful of the cold tart liquid.

'It's all probably moot anyway,' Mae said, sighing afresh. 'That man is from a whole other dimension. One where men date nuclear physicists who model in their spare time. Or he's gay.'

'Not gay,' Paige said, remembering the way his gaze had caressed her face. The certainty he'd been moving closer to her the whole ride, inch by big hot inch. Jet lag or no, there'd been something there. She took a deep breath and said, 'Anyway. It doesn't matter either way. A man who flirts with a woman holding a wedding dress ought to be neutered.'

'Well, my sweet,' said Mae, perking up, 'you'll have the chance to tell him so. Because he's coming this way.'

Gabe had been about to leave when he'd seen her.

Well, he'd seen her dinner companion first—a redhead with wild curls and no qualms about staring at strangers. After which he'd noticed his fine and fidgety neighbour's blonde waves tumbling down a back turned emphatically in his direction. If she'd given him a smile and a wave he might well have waved and gone home. But the fact that the woman he'd planned to ignore was ignoring him right on back tugged at his perverse gene and sent him walking her way.

'Well, if it isn't Miss Eighth Floor,' he said, resting a hand on the back of her chair.

Paige turned, her eyebrows raised, her smile cool. But the second her deep blue eyes locked onto his, his blood thickened, his lungs got tight, and he felt a sudden surge of affection for the hard floor of his room.

Hitchcock be damned, he thought as the memory of those cool blonde waves tickling his chest as she'd ridden him in his convertible slammed into his head. It might only have been a dream but his libido clearly didn't give a lick. 'When I said I'd see you around I wasn't expecting it to be quite so soon.'

'Living in the same building we'll be bound to run into one another.'

'Lucky us.' He gave her a smile, the kind he knew gave off all the right signals. Her eyes flared, but she physically pulled her reaction back. In fact from her pale pink fingernails gripping the table, to the ends of her gorgeously tousled hair, she screamed high maintenance. Complication. Trouble.

And yet the smile tugged higher at the corners of his mouth.

Maybe it was the challenge. Maybe it was the dream. Maybe it was that he suddenly had time on his hands, time he'd rather spend in doing than thinking. But as Gabe looked into those hot and cold blue eyes he knew he was going to get to know this woman.

A loud clearing of the throat sent them both looking to Paige's friend.

Paige said, 'Gabe Hamilton, this is my friend Mae. Her fiancé, Clint.'

Leaning across the table to shake hands with enthusiasm, Mae said, 'I hear you've just flown in from overseas.'

When the table shook and Mae scrunched up her face, Gabe got the feeling she'd been duly kicked under the table. So Little Miss Cool had been talking about him to her friends, had she? Perhaps this would be easier than he thought. Though rather than that taking the edge off the challenge, the energy inside coiled tighter still.

He sourced a spare chair at the next table and

dragged it over, sliding it next to Paige, who pretended she'd suddenly found a mark on her dinner plate fascinating.

'Brazil,' he said to Mae, pressing his toes into the floor as Paige sat straight as an arrow in the seat beside him. 'I'm just back from Brazil.'

'Seriously?' said Mae. 'Hear that, Paige? Gabe's been to Brazil.'

Paige glared at her friend. 'Thanks, Mae. I did hear.'

Mae leant her chin on her palm as she asked, 'Back for good, then?'

'Not,' he said. Not that he was about to tell these nice people that given the choice he'd rather be neck deep in piranha-infested waters than stay in their home town. 'Here on business for a few days.'

'Pity,' said Mae, while Paige said nothing. Those bedroom eyes of hers remained steadfastly elsewhere. Until Mae added, 'Paige has a total thing for Brazil.'

'Does she, now?'

At the low note that had crept into his voice, Paige's eyes finally flickered to his. He smiled back, giving her a silent 'hi' with his eyes. She saw it too. Her eyes widened, all simmering heat trapped beneath the cool surface, and her chest rose and fell at the same time as his, as if she was breathing with him.

Gabe's libido, which had been warming up nicely since the moment he'd spied her, went off like a rocket. He gripped the back of her chair, his thumb mere millimetres from the dip between her shoulders. When Paige breathed deep, arching away from his almost touch, her nostrils flaring, her throat working, he swore beneath his breath.

'Why, yes,' said Mae cheerfully, seemingly oblivious to the sexual tension near pulsing between her table-mates. 'In fact she's spent the past few months trying to convince her boss she has to shoot their summer catalogue there.'

'Really?' Gabe said, dragging his gaze to her friend in an effort to keep himself decent. 'So what kind of work does Paige do?'

'I'm brand manager for a home-wares retailer,' Paige shot back, a distinct huskiness now lighting her voice. *Oh, yeah, this was going to be fun.* 'Most of next summer's range is Brazilian. In feel if not in actuality.' Then, as if the words were being pulled from her with pliers, 'And what were you doing in Brazil?'

If he'd been in need of a bucket of water to cool the trouble brewing in his pants, Paige asking about his work was a fine alternative. He'd learned the hard way that the less people knew about his business, the better. *What big information you have! All the better to screw you with, my dear.* 'This time around, coffee,' he allowed. 'You like coffee?'

'Coffee?' She blinked, the change of subject catching her off guard. She shifted till she was facing him a little more. Her eyes now flitting between his, the push and pull of attraction working up the same energy he'd felt at their first meeting. Then she slid her bottom lip between her teeth, leaving it moist and plump as she said, 'Depends who's making it.'

Gabe felt the ground beneath him dip and sway as it had in the lift and he gripped the back of her chair for dear life. *Vertigo,* he thought, *definitely vertigo.* Hitchcock had been a glutton for punishment to keep going back to his twitchy blondes. Yet Gabe made no move to leave, so what did that make him?

'Why coffee?' Mae asked.

'Hmm?'

'The reason you were in Brazil. Do you grow it? Pick it? Drink it? Brew it?'

Gabe paused again, calculating. But the deal was done. He'd gone over every full stop, met every employee, vetted every business practice to make sure the product line was legitimate and above reproach. And profitable, of course. Nothing, and nobody, could ruin it now.

'I'm investing in it. Or in a mob called Bean There, to be more specific,' he said.

But it was too late. Paige had sensed his hesitation and, for whatever reason, her knees slid away from his and back under the table. Hot and cold? The woman ran from fire to frost quicker than he could keep up.

At that point Gabe seriously considered cutting his losses. But at his heart Gabe was a shark. When he got his teeth in something it took a hell of a lot for him to let go. It was why he was the best at what he did, why he'd never met a deal he couldn't close. She didn't know it yet, but the longer she sat there shutting him out, the deeper she sank her hook beneath his ribs.

A voice from across the table said, 'Oh, I love those places! Those little hole-in-the-wall joints, right? One guy and a coffee machine.'

'That's the ones.'

'Ooh, how exciting,' Mae said, 'insider information! From our very own corporate pirate.'

Gabe flinched so hard he bit his tongue. It was as

though the woman had the book on which buttons to press to make his jewels up and shrivel. 'It's common knowledge,' he avowed, 'so feel free to spread the word. The more money they make, the more steak dinners for me.'

Clearly the time had come to retreat and regroup. He pulled himself to standing.

'Stay!' said Mae.

'Thanks, but no. Beauty sleep to catch up on.'

He looked to Paige to check if she was even half as moved by his imminent departure, only to find her sitting primly with her fingers clasped together as if she didn't give a hoot. Yet her gaze had other ideas. Beginning somewhere in the region of his fly, it did a slow slide up his torso, pausing for the briefest moments on his chest, his neck, his mouth, before landing on his eyes.

'Friday,' he heard himself say in a voice that was pure testosterone. 'Housewarming party at mine. You're all welcome.'

'We'll be there,' said Mae.

Gabe reached out to shake Mae's hand. Then Clint's. He saved Paige for last.

'Paige,' he said, and he lifted her hand into his. His dream had been wrong on that point at the very least. Her hand was as warm as if she'd been lying in the sun. As for her eyes... As if touching him had unleashed all that she'd been trying to hold back, desire flooded them, then exploded in his chest like a bonfire, before settling as a hot ache in his groin.

Damn.

She pulled her hand away. Her brow furrowing, as

if she wasn't sure what had just happened. He knew. And hell if he didn't want more.

'Friday,' he said, waiting until she nodded. Then he shot the table a salute before walking away, his entire body coiled in discomfort, his field of vision a pinprick in a field of red mist as blood pounded through his body way too fast.

He headed back to his apartment. To his hard floor. The ache lingering deep in his gut. And this time as he stared at the ceiling in his big empty bedroom, sleep eluded him.

He wondered how his neighbour might react if he showed up at her door asking for a bed for the night, carrying his box of doughnuts and wearing nothing but boxer shorts and a smile. The only thing keeping him from finding out was her patent determination to remain cool. If he read her even slightly wrong, boxer shorts might be not quite enough protection.

THREE

Later that night, when the lift doors closed several minutes after Paige had pressed the button for the eighth floor, she leant against the wall, getting herself comfortable for the ride ahead of her.

The second she closed her eyes, the picture projected onto the backs of her lids was the view of Gabe Hamilton as he'd walked away. All long strong legs and loping sexy strides. The thought of him made her tingle all over. Like static, only...hotter.

As it turned out, whatever she thought of Gabe Hamilton's scruples about flirting with a possibly engaged woman, she hadn't imagined the spark. It was there, in the directness of his gaze. The purpose in his smile. He knew he was gorgeous and wasn't above using it to get what he wanted. And if she had even half a sense about such things, he wanted her.

Paige crossed her legs at the ankle and slid her thumb between her front teeth and nibbled for all she was worth.

She'd never been one of those girls who went after

men who looked as if they sinned a dozen times a day and twice on Sundays. Sure, she could appreciate the appeal. The desire to tame the untameable. But she'd seen the emotional destruction a man with that kind of concentrated charm left in his wake. And while she wasn't a big believer in happy endings, more than that she was determined never to act in such a way as to have an unhappy one.

Unfortunately, she hadn't dated any good guys of late either. The why of it niggled at a shadowy corner of her brain, as if it should be more obvious. But while her head filled with thoughts of Gabe Hamilton, and his hot hand and hotter eyes, she was finding it hard to think straight at all.

She pulled herself upright, shook out her hands, and paced around the lift.

The sorry truth was, she'd met enough 'good guys' who turned out to be jerks in the end anyway. So wouldn't it be better to know a guy was trouble from the outset? Wouldn't it be easier to protect herself if she knew up front exactly what she was in for? Wouldn't it be something to let go and open up to all that sinful, seductive intensity just once?

Her eyes scrunched tight and she stopped pacing.

Despite evidence to the contrary, Gabe Hamilton didn't seem like a jerk. He seemed...focused. Sexy as all get out. More than a little bit intimidating. And by his own admission, he was only in town for a bit. Which was a plus. Maybe the biggest plus of all. She wasn't after a relationship with the guy. Just a safe place to dip her toes into the dating pool. A kiss. Maybe a little messing about. Or a good and proper tumble.

She sucked in a deep breath and let it go.

Anyway, she didn't have to decide that night. She had till Friday at the very least to think about it, so long as they never shared the lift in that time. Not that it had ever done right by her before.

When the lift made its first stop she twirled her hair over one shoulder, stifled a yawn, glanced at the number to check which floor besides the eighth she'd landed on, then realised the lift had taken her to the top. To the penthouse.

She slowly stood to attention, her hands tight on her purse in an attempt to get a grip on the sensual wave rising through her knowing Gabe Hamilton was close. And with everything she had she willed the lift to descend.

But the lift being the lift, the doors slid open, and stayed open, leaving her standing staring into a large dark entrance boasting two shiny black double doors leading to the only apartment on the floor, one of which bumped as the handle twisted.

Paige shrank to the back of the lift, but there was no hiding. Every last wisp of air bled from her lungs as Gabe stepped through the doorway.

He looked up, saw her, and stopped. A muscle worked in his jaw. It was a testament to how her senses were working nineteen to the dozen that she even noticed that tiny movement, considering what the guy was wearing. Or not wearing, to be more precise.

Pyjama bottoms. Long, soft, grey-checked pyjama bottoms. And nothing else. After that it was like a freeway collision inside her head, the way the gorgeous bits of him piled on top of one another. The deep tan that went all over. The large bare feet. The hair, all mussed and rugged. Arms that looked strong enough to lift a small car. A wholly masculine chest with the kind of muscle definition no mere mortal had the right to possess. And a happy trail of dark hair arrowing beneath his pyjama bottoms...

'Paige?' he said, his devil-deep voice putting her knees on notice.

'Hey,' she croaked back.

'I heard the lift.'

'And here it is.' Going for unflappable, she cocked a hip and waved a hand towards the open doors like a game-show hostess. She failed the moment the heat rising through her body pinked across her cheeks.

A hint of a smile gathered in Gabe's dark eyes, tilting his gorgeous mouth. 'Did you want me for something?'

'Did I want you—? No. *No.*' She laughed only slightly hysterically. 'I was heading home, but the lift, it—'

'Brought you here of its own accord.'

'It's contrary that way.'

'So you've said,' he said, planting his feet and crossing his arms across his chest, a broad, brown, beautiful mass of rises and falls that brought a flash flood to the desert that had been her mouth.

Paige dragged her eyes to the huge starburst on the ceiling as she said, 'It's late and you must have things to do, bags to unpack, sleep to catch up on.'

He slowly shook his head. 'I'm used to living out of a bag. And for some reason I'm not all that tired right now.'

'I could be here a while.'

He leaned against the doorjamb. 'Or you could come in.'

The blood thundered so hard and fast through her she couldn't be sure she'd heard him right. 'Come in?'

'I can tell you everything I know about Brazil.'

Paige blinked. Simply unable to find the words to—

'And I have doughnuts.'

And at that she laughed. Loud. Nervous energy pouring from her in waves. 'Well, that's original. I mean, I've been offered "coffee" before of course. Even a good old-fashioned nightcap on occasion. But never doughnuts.'

He watched her, all dark, and leaning and so much man. Her mouth now watering like Niagara Falls, she swallowed again before saying, 'What is a nightcap anyway? Sounds like it should be one of those Wee Willie Winkie hats with the pompom on the end—'

'Paige.'

'I...' Her eyes slid to his naked chest as if they'd stayed too long away. 'I feel overdressed for doughnuts.'

'Only one way to fix that.'

She realised then that he'd moved aside so that the way through his open front door was clear. Inviting.

Her body waved towards the open lift doors, gripped with a desire to step across that threshold and into the arms of one big hot male, but she caught herself at the last second. She couldn't. Could she? She'd met him that morning, for Pete's sake. Knew nothing about him other than his name, address and occupation— Okay, so that was pretty standard. As for the way he made her feel—as if she were melting from the inside out—by looking at her?

The lift binged, the doors began to close, and Paige slipped through the gap, the bump and hum of the lift descending without her echoing through her shaking limbs. Other than that the dark foyer was perfectly quiet. No music. Just the sound of her shaky breath sliding past her lips.

She'd have a doughnut. Get to know him a little. Maybe even grab him at the last for a goodnight kiss. She could handle a guy like Gabe for one night if that was what it took to find her dating legs again; legs that wobbled like a marionette's as she made her way to his door.

She held her breath as she slipped past him but there was no avoiding that complex masculine scent radiating from his warm naked skin.

Inside, the apartment was darker still. When he went towards the raised kitchen, Paige headed in the opposite direction where cloud-shrouded moonlight spilled through the wall of ceiling-to-floor windows. And he hadn't been lying when he'd said there was nothing to unpack. In fact there wasn't much of anything at all.

No lamps, only the light of an open laptop on the kitchen bench. No pictures on the walls. Not even a big-screen TV. Just a couch, a long, sleek L-shaped thing that could fit twenty. And it looked out over the stunning water view, as if the inside of the apartment was irrelevant.

Which maybe, to him, it was. In her experience a man who refused to stamp his own personality on a place wasn't connected to it. Or those living in it with him. Hence the unrestrained frippery of the home she grew up in. If a home was where the heart was, then Gabe Hamilton's heart was most definitely not in that apartment. Probably not even in her home city. And while in the past that would have been enough to turn her on her heel without looking back, her heart began to race.

'Not a big fan of decor?' she asked, glancing across to find him in the raised kitchen where a single muted down-light now played over his naked torso, making the absolute most of his warm brown skin. He loomed over a huge white box that did, in fact, contain doughnuts. 'Or furnishings in general?'

He looked around as if he hadn't noticed how bare the place was. 'I don't spend my weekends antiquing, if that's what you mean.'

'You don't have to go that far, but you could do with a dining table. Some kitchen stools. A throw cushion or two.'

'I'd bet my left foot that no man ever looked back on his life and regretted a lack of throw cushions,' he rumbled.

'But they're like garnish on a dinner plate. You don't need it to make the meal, but that splash of colour makes your mouth water all the same.'

To that he said nothing, just watched her across the darkness, and her own mouth had never watered as much in her entire life.

'Is it just me, or is it hot in here?' she asked, peeling off her shirred blazer, her knobbly scarf, and throwing them over the back of a couch.

'Air-con's on heat blast. I'm acclimatising.'

Her eyes fell onto a plate of doughnuts he was piling high. She edged towards the scent of sugar. And him. 'Turn the heat down and put on a sweater. Much more comfortable.'

'For who?'

For her clearly. She'd been inside his place for less than two minutes and already a drop of sweat slid between her shoulder blades, trickled down her spine, and pooled in the dent at the bottom of her back.

As for him? His gaze lingered on her cream silk top, hovered over the minuscule spaghetti straps, then swept down her bare arms. Paige fought the urge to cross her arms across her chest, as even in the sweltering room her nipples contracted to aching peaks.

'Nah,' he said as his eyes moseyed back up to hers, 'I like the heat.'

Leaving the doughnuts to the elements, Gabe edged around the island, his dark eyes locked onto her. Heart pounding, she backed up a step, and her backside hit the couch.

'Would you prefer I turn it down?' he asked, his voice dropping as he neared.

God, no, she thought. By the twitch at the corner of his beautiful mouth, she realised she'd clearly said it out loud. *Bad habit. Must break.*

He moved closer, and, breathing deep, she caught his wholly masculine scent that made her certain he could change a tyre, and build a fire, and wrestle a shark all before breakfast and not break a sweat.

And she knew. There would be no doughnuts that night. There would be no lines drawn, or contracts agreed upon. Her world contracted until all she knew was moonlight, heat, breath, her throbbing pulse. And Gabe. Half naked, his dark gaze searing into hers.

Then, right when she thought she might die from the tension coiling within her, he took one last long step and his big hand was in her hair, and his hot mouth was on hers.

Explosions went off behind her eyes, beneath her skin, deep in her belly until her whole body was awash with heat that had nothing to do with the sweltering air.

Her hands were in his hair gouging tracks in the lush softness. Her leg was wrapped around his. Her body arcing into him as every part of her that could meld with his did.

She felt his smile against her mouth. A smile of pure and utter conquest. She nipped at his bottom lip. *Take that.*

He stilled, all that strength bunching, waiting, compounding. In the stillness his heat beat against her skin. The energy coursing through his veins found a matching beat in hers. Every sense was on a delectable high.

When the wait for retribution became too much, she rolled against him. Softly. Fitted herself along his length. Purposefully. Slid her hands to the back of his head, and her tongue across his bottom lip, tasting the tender spot she'd bitten.

This, she thought. This was what she'd needed. This raw release. Who needed promises? Who needed commitment? Of all times for her friend to pop into her head, this was not a winner. Clint joined Mae as they smiled at one another in that gooey way they had when they thought nobody was watching. In fact, they didn't really care who was watching, they were too busy watching one another.

Paige shook her head in an effort to remove the image from her mind, and the usual dull ache it had created deep in her belly.

As if he sensed her retreat, Gabe closed his big strong arms around her, wrapping her in heat and muscle and might. He pressed her back and kissed her slow and deep until she was nothing bar a flood of sensation pouring hot and thick through her whole body. His scent curled itself about her, warm, spicy, mouth-watering, until she couldn't remember what her mouth tasted like before it tasted like him.

This. The word whispered through her again.

And things only got better from there for a really long time. As he found the sweet spot below her right ear, sucking her skin into his hot mouth. The hollow at the base of her neck with his tongue. The line of lace where the edge of her bra met swollen sensitive skin. Until her mind was a haze. Her body pure vibration.

She groaned in frustration as his lips were gone from hers, but then his arm slid beneath her legs and he lifted her as if she weighed nothing. She wrapped her arms around his shoulders and held on tight, her breath shooting from her lungs as light, bright, startled laughter.

When her eyes found his, dangerous and intense, the laughter dried up in her throat, the pleasure of it trickling down to her toes.

She bumped in his arms as he kicked open what

must have been the bedroom door. Then he stopped so fast she gripped on tighter so as not to fly out of his arms.

'Dammit,' he said. Followed by a whole slew of words worthy of any pirate.

'Problem?'

He slid her down his body, his hardness giving her no doubt he was as deep in this thing as she was. Then he took her by the shoulders and turned her so that she could see into his bedroom.

It was huge, half the size of her whole apartment. Gorgeous window mouldings and cornices, with another fabulous art deco sun-burst in the centre of the high ceiling. Occupational hazard, it took her half a second to imagine a reading lamp and great chair in the near corner. A small antique desk with enough room for his laptop below the wide window. Lush dark curtains pooling on the shiny floor. None of which were there.

But decor and character weren't the only things the room was lacking.

It had no bed.

A small sound of desperation escaped her lips as her eyes roved quickly over the scrunched-up blankets on the floor, none of which looked terribly conducive to the kind of action her poor neglected body was screaming for.

She swore beneath her breath. Or at least she thought she had. The rumble of laughter at her back told her she'd said it out loud. Again.

Then his hand slid around her waist, tucked beneath her top, and found her sensitive stomach. She melted against him, against the hardness pressed against her backside. He swept her hair aside and his teeth grazed her shoulder and if she hadn't pressed her thighs together she'd have orgasmed on the spot.

She spun in his arms, her hands finding his firm chest. His body filled her view, blocking out any light that dared come between them. His face was all darkness and shadows, his skin like a furnace, his scent like pure testosterone. Instinct had her swaying back, only to find herself up against the doorjamb.

'Gabe...' Paige said, her spine merging with the line of the doorway.

His hand landed on the doorjamb above her head. She breathed out. Slow, shaky, every ounce of oxygen leaving her body until she was weak with desire. Heat licking and trembling at her core. She couldn't feel her feet. Could feel the beat of his heart against her palms all the way in the backs of her knees.

Her chest felt tight, her lungs dysfunctional. She wasn't sure how much longer she could hang onto her self-control. But if she pulled back now, how long till she had such a chance again? If she turned away from *this*, she might as well buy a cat, get a blue rinse and be done with men for ever.

She curled her fingers and traced her nails through the crisp dark hair of his chest. Pressed her lips gently to his flat nipple, before tracing it with her tongue. Her hands, getting greedy now, roved over the bumps of his six-pack, the hard muscles at his hips, over what turned out to be a damn fine example of male backside.

Something close to a roar escaped Gabe's mouth

as his fingers curled into her hair and tugged, sending her head sliding down the vertical strip of wood. Then his mouth found hers, any gentleness or exploration gone, his lips and tongue making a joke of any last resistance she might have had.

He tucked his fingers beneath the strap of her top, sending it cascading down her arm, revealing the lacy half-cup of her bra. His eyes, dark as night, watched as his palm cupped her breast, then his thumb ran over the dark centre. Chills running up and down her body, she pressed her feet into the floor and she bit her lip so as not to cry out.

His hand found her hip, his thumb swirling over her belly button. Then before she knew it her jeans were unbuttoned, the zip sliding open one tooth at a time. Paige's hands went to Gabe's hips, grabbing on for dear life as his big hand slid inside her pants, cupping her. Then he slid a slow, strong finger along the seam of her underwear.

She bucked as a shot of the most exquisite pleasure pierced her, blocking out every other sensation.

Then his mouth was on hers again, taking her blissful agony and doubling it. Trebling it. Turning her thoughts to mere threads swirling in a wash of liquid heat as a finger curled beneath the hem of her underwear, dipped inside her, sending wave after wave of shock and awe through her.

Her body no longer her own, she strained towards him. The perfect insistent slide of his finger. Then two. Melting from the inside out as blood roared in her ears, all sensation rushed to her centre, and, with a cry stifled as her mouth pressed against his shoulder, she came. A riot of hot waves buffeting her from scalp to toes, again and again, before finally diffusing to a warm delicious hum.

Her skin was slick with sweat. Her lips tasted of salt. Her knuckles ached from the clench of her fingers at Gabe's hips.

Her eyes opened sluggishly as her top slid back up her torso, at the scrape of a fingernail as her strap hooked back over her shoulder. No. No! What was he doing? Even through the haze of afterglow she knew they weren't *done*. Not by half!

Her focus landed on his eyes to find them lit by a slow burn that turned her mouth dry. She traced her thumbs into the waistline of his pants and he stopped her, his expression almost pained. His voice was subterranean when he asked, 'Do you have protection?'

And she felt the floor drop out from under her.

It had been months, literally, since she'd needed a condom. Or even thought to put it on her shopping list; that was how dry her spell had been. She was on the pill of course, but she'd known this guy less than a day.

She must have looked as disappointed as she felt as Gabe's forehead thunked against the wood, his breath shooting hot and hard over her shoulder, creating fresh goose bumps in its wake. 'The closest chemist is three blocks from here.'

'If I go outside in this state I'll be arrested.'

'Or there's the stacked brunette on six.'

With palpable effort, Gabe pulled back. His dark eyes connecting with hers, the intensity coming at her making her knees buckle. 'What about her?'

'She looks the kind of girl who might have a permanent stash of such...accessories.'

After a few moments of quiet, Gabe burst out laughing. 'Not quite the impression I want to make on the neighbours, door-knocking at one in the morning with a hard-on and a request for condoms.'

Condoms, she thought. *Plural. Good God.*

'No,' she said, licking her suddenly dry lips. 'I suppose not. Even if you are only in town for a little while?'

Gabe's dark eyes seared into her as if he was actually considering it. Then after one hard breath in and out, he took her by one finger and dragged her in his wake, away from the cruel temptation of his under-utilised bedroom and back into his big under-decorated home where he gathered her clothes.

'Gabe?' she said, half apology, half despair.

He shooshed her with a glance that told her he was barely controlling himself as it was. She bit her lip and kept quiet.

Once at the lift he redressed her until she had a semblance of decency. 'In case the lift stops on another man's floor,' he said, the gleam in his eyes making it clear he didn't believe her story for a second. 'Wouldn't want him to get the wrong idea.'

'But—'

The lift opened. His jaw tightened and Paige was sure he was about to kiss her again. Her lips opened, her breath hitched, her skin came over all hot and tingly. But he turned her on the spot and gave her a little shove inside. 'Scram. Before I start something neither one of us will be able to stop.'

Compared with his apartment, the inside of the

lift was freezing cold. She crossed her arms across her chest to hold in the warmth. To hold in the delicious fizzing in her blood. The wonderful heaviness between her legs.

What to say? *Sorry? Thanks? See you around?* In the end neither of them said anything, they just watched each other as the lift doors closed.

She slumped against the wall—her legs no longer able to support her—slapped a hand over her eyes and shook her head. What had *happened*? She'd broken her drought, that was what. And how! As the lift took her to the lobby and back a half-dozen times Paige relived every hot, rash second of it to make sure.

When the lift finally opened at her floor, she breathed out a long shuddering sigh of relief. Considering how her day had begun, she couldn't possibly have hoped to negate that disaster so soon. But she had.

Hopefully now her life could get back to normal.

FOUR

—

Paige's phone rang, but no matter how hard she reached, how hard she tried, it was never enough. She couldn't connect.

She woke up with a start, her heart thumping in her chest, her legs entangled in a mess of sheets, to find light pouring through her bedroom window. A quick glance at her bedside clock told her it was after ten. Once she realised it was a Sunday she relaxed. Wow, she hadn't slept in that late in—

The buzzing of her landline told her she hadn't dreamt that part at least.

She reached out, grabbed the phone, lay back on her bed with the back of her hand over her eyes to block out the light. Expecting it to be her mum, she sighed, 'Hiya.'

'Sleep well?'

Words became impossible as her mouth fell wide open. She had to swallow, twice, before saying, 'Gabe?'

'Making sure you got home okay last night.'

Her head was spinning. How did he get her number?

She hadn't given it to him. He'd looked her up? He'd looked her up! *Oh, calm down. It doesn't mean anything. He's just being gentlemanly.* Though what he'd done to her up against the doorjamb the night before was so far from gentlemanly she had to cross her legs to keep from suffering a relapse.

'Paige?'

'I hardly had to brave the night. I'm four floors down.'

'As I well know.' The heat in Gabe's voice had Paige sliding deeper under her sheets. Until he added, 'By way of a lift that, according to you, is contrary.'

'You still think I'm making it up, don't you?'

'Don't get me wrong, I'm not complaining. In fact I've developed a soft spot for the thing.'

She could all but see his seductive smile down the phone. Feel his warm breath on her neck. His hot hands on her skin. How had she convinced herself a night with Gabe Hamilton would be enough? Maybe it would have been, if either of them had come with protection. And maybe she'd turn into a monkey at the next full moon.

Whatever might have been, after last night he'd been left wanting, and she was left wanting more. And not just getting out there and dating again more. Him more. Big dark Gabe Hamilton more. That was what came of diving in head first when she'd meant to test the water with a tentative toe. But it was too late to think about what she should have done. She was in this thing now. Why not make the most of it?

'Where are you?' she asked. Her body began to feel

hot and soft by turns at the hope he would say he was outside her door.

'Why?'

'No reason.'

'Liar,' he rumbled. Not only did the man have a voice that could send a nun into a fit of hot trembles, he knew what to do with it. 'I'm at Customs. Tearing the place down in search of my bed.'

'Couldn't sleep?'

'Not so much. You?'

'I slept fine.' Deep, dreamy, delicious.

The low notes of Gabe's laughter vibrated down the phone. And Paige bit her lip so as not to say anything else incriminating.

'Glad to hear you're safe and sound. And well slept. Now I've gotta see a man about a bed. See you 'round, Eighth Floor.' And then he was gone.

Paige pressed the phone to her hot ear a moment longer before she let her arm flop sideways, the phone dangling from her hand. She stared at the ceiling, at the bouncing blobs of sunlight reflecting off the prism dangling from the corner of her dressing-table mirror.

He'd checked to see if she made it home. Which was actually quite lovely. Kind of a good guy thing to do, in fact. But then he'd made no noise about when, or even if, she'd see him again before Friday's party. Which was a decidedly bad boy thing to do.

She rolled onto her tummy and pressed her face into her pillow. If only he were outside her door with a condom tucked in the back pocket of his old jeans. Then he could have his wicked way with her, and they'd be even, and that would be that. Perhaps. Probably not.

It was a Sunday, she had nowhere else to be, so she closed her eyes and pictured herself flinging open her front door to find him standing there after all, though this time in her head he wore black leather trousers, a loose white shirt open to the navel, an eye-patch. He was so big and tall he'd fill her small kitchen—

Her eyes flew open and she sat up with a start as she remembered the wedding dress in its fluorescent bag still hanging over her dining chair.

She rubbed the heels of her palms against her eye socket and breathed out hard. Then she caught a glimpse of herself in the dressing-table mirror. Her eyes were smudged with old eyeliner, her hair a scrambled mess. And her mouth? It tasted like three-week-old bread.

Looking as she looked, with a wedding dress in her kitchen, hearing one note of that voice and she would still have let him into her apartment in half a second flat. No, she would have dragged him in. Had she completely lost her self-control?

That was that. Until his party Friday she was using the stairs.

As Gabe leaned against the wall of the lift transporting him silently to the fifteenth floor offices of BonaVenture Capital he couldn't help comparing it with the one at the Botany Apartments. Light, bright, luxuriously spacious and prompt as this one was, it hadn't the added benefit of having deposited pure temptation in the shape of a leggy blonde at his door two nights before. He knew which he preferred, hands down.

He was quite sure this casual dalliance would end

up being a most welcome postscript to the unwelcome trip. Casual being the key word.

He liked women. Downright adored some of them. He'd been raised by a strong woman—his gran, after his parents died a week before his tenth birthday—so he respected the hell out of them. But his work kept him on the move, which made casual more workable. That, and the fact that the one and only time he'd attempted a hearts and roses relationship he'd been burned to a crisp.

He shifted his stance, but the discomfort that had settled over him remained. He preferred not to look back to that time. It was a big black hole in his past with the capability to suck him in if he gave it half a chance. Being back in Melbourne, heading into the BonaVenture offices where it had all come to a head made it nearby impossible *not* to remember, but he was determined to try.

And if losing himself in the warm, willing arms of Paige Danforth every now and then helped, then who was he to argue?

He was rubbing at the bite marks she'd left on his shoulder when the lift dinged. He pressed his feet into the floor and held his breath, only to lose it in a rush when the doors opened to an expansive foyer with a shining dark wooden floor, blood-red walls, and sunlight seeming to pour from every corner of the place even though he couldn't see a single window.

He glanced back at the floor number to make sure lifts all over the city hadn't suddenly gone mad.

It was only when he looked up that he saw a sign twice as long as he was tall advertising *BonaVenture*

Capital in elegant white type that he was sure he was in the right place. This was his company, only nothing like it had been when he'd last been in Melbourne. Two years before? Three? Now he remembered Nate carrying on about paint swatches during a lot of emails and calls at one point. He'd agreed to Nate spending whatever he liked on the refit so long as he didn't have to read another memo about the critical difference between Egg White Omelette and Alabaster Dream. Whichever way Nate had gone, it worked.

'Wow,' he bit out, shocked laughter rumbling in his chest.

Shrugging his laptop bag higher on his shoulder, Gabe slowly walked through the foyer dodging the hive of men and women in sharp suits bustling back and forth to and from hallways hidden away to the sides. To think it had been less than ten years since they'd started their venture capital firm with Nate's trust fund, Gabe's hard-earned savings from every job he'd had since he was twelve years old, and a business plan mapped out on a handful of beer napkins in a dark corner of their favourite pub while their college mates downed shots at the same table.

He remembered like it was yesterday, walking through the city the next morning, while the grey city turned gold with the magic touch of sunlight, feeling as if his life was finally about to begin. As if he literally had the whole world at his feet. As if brilliance was within his grasp.

And then a smidge under three years later he'd nearly lost it all. And he'd spent every second of the last seven years of his life making up for it.

He pressed his boots into the expensive floor and for the first time since that time he let himself wonder if they might have finally pulled through.

'Buddy!' Nate said, appearing from nowhere as if by osmosis. He must have noticed the surprise on Gabe's face as he laughed loud enough to turn heads. 'So what do you think? Gorgeous right?'

'Egg White Omelette?' he asked, pointing a thumb at the company name.

'Plain old White,' Nate said.

'Who'd have thought?'

'Want to see your office?'

'Hell, yeah,' Gabe said. Though for half a second he wondered if he deserved anything more than a hole in the wall considering how often he used the place. But Nate's excitement soon had him feeling a glimmer of anticipation at what lay beyond the doors Nate had led him to. 'So what does a partner in a schmancy joint like this get for his buck?'

Nate grinned as he opened the doors with a flourish to reveal a corner office big enough to host a pool tournament. Huge gleaming glass desk. Acres of lush dark carpet so thick you could swim in it. And that was it.

Gabe found himself forced to school his face so as not to show his intense disappointment at its lack of... something. Nate had decked it out exactly the same as his apartment. Bare. Static. Distinctly lacking *garnish*.

Nate slapped him on the back. 'I'll give you a minute to settle in. Take a lap or ten. Spin around like Julie Andrews on the hilltop.'

Then he was out of the door, leaving Gabe alone in the big empty room.

Feeling tight and antsy, he whipped the beanie off his head and ran his fingers hard through his hair, realising it needed a cut. At the rustle of his leather jacket sleeve it occurred to him he was probably the only person on the entire floor not in a suit.

'And this is why I don't come back here,' he told the walls, which could only be Light Grey. Turned out slapping on a fresh coat of paint didn't nullify his history with the place after all. He could feel it pressing in on him from every angle.

The only time he hadn't felt the pressure was when he was with Paige. Deep in the rush he got when a blush rose up her elegant neck. In pounding lust every time he witnessed the love-affair her teeth had with her bottom lip. Drunk on the taste of her sweet skin. Unleashed by the bottomless wells of desire clouding her big blue eyes.

That was that. When he wasn't doing what he came to Melbourne to do, he'd bury himself to the hilt in a most agreeable leggy blonde. And once the job was over, he wouldn't be seen for dust.

His relief was short-lived when he saw Nate's arms were filled with a pile of daunting-looking binders. Throwing them on the desk with a hearty thump, Nate said, 'No need to tell you, I'm sure, how hush-hush this has to be.'

Gabe merely stared at Nate while he waited for the irony to sink in that he was telling that to the one man who'd learned that lesson the hard way.

'Right,' Nate said, with the good grace to look sheepish. 'Now read up. And then I need your take. Are we going to list BonaVenture on the stock market, or what?'

* * *

Paige walked along the promenade, the heels of her ankle boots clacking rhythmically against the cobblestones, her long skirt clinging to her tights with static, her wool scarf flapping behind her. No wonder she loved winter. It had been nearly two days since her sexual jump start, and still every shift of fabric on her skin felt like a caress.

Her stomach rumbled expectantly at the scent of warm food flowing from the open doors of the run of restaurants below the apartment buildings lining the waterside. What the heck? She'd order The Brasserie's melt-in-your-mouth steak and chips to go.

It had been a good day. The girl who delivered morning tea had brought her favourite raspberry and white-chocolate muffins. The first product for Ménage à Moi's summer line arrived into the warehouse and looked gorgeous; all luscious fabrics and rich decadent colours, as sexy and sensuous as Carnival itself.

In fact she couldn't remember enjoying her work so much in a good while. The past few months she'd found herself growing frustrated there too, hence the hyper-motivation to get the Brazil proposal off the ground. Discontent seemed to have crept into more parts of her life than she'd realised, which made no sense. Her life was *exactly* as she'd always planned for it to be. A great apartment, a great job, a great social life, and all of it on her own terms. What more could she want?

She shook her head. What mattered was that things were looking up. At work, and in the bedroom if the number of men who'd smiled at her that day was anything to go by. She'd felt so many eyes on her it was as if she were surrounded by a cloud of flirtatious energy. She'd smiled back but kept on walking. Happy to take her time, now her wheels were back on the track.

Her mobile beeped. For a brief second she imagined a naughty message from Gabe, not that she'd heard from him since that phone call the morning before. The one that had left her with so much idle sexual energy she'd cleaned her entire kitchen, oven included.

Until she remembered he didn't have her mobile number, as only her home number was listed. He didn't even know which apartment was hers as far as she knew, only her floor. Enough to track her down if he wanted to. Which in nearly forty-eight hours he hadn't.

Why hadn't he? Unless his phone call the day before had really been about making sure she'd made it home all right and nothing more.

She shook her head again. They weren't dating. They were barely even lovers. She'd taken this thing as it had come so far and would continue to do so until it faded. Or he left. And that was that.

Nevertheless, when she checked her phone it was with a level of anticipation that left her knees quaking so much she had to pull over to the side of the cobbled path. When she saw the message was from her mum Paige's good mood took a little trip sideways.

Miss you, darling, the message read. Paige grimaced. She knew that tone. It was the one where her mum was feeling sorry for herself, and wondering, even all these years later, if divorcing Paige's dad had been the right thing to do.

Miss you too! Paige tapped into her phone, looking

up every second or two to make sure nobody barrelled into her. *Want me to come over for dinner?*

You're busy. You probably have plans.

Paige bit her lip at the thought of the steak and chips for one she had planned. But her day really had been so good. And if she had any intention of retaining the new lightness in her step she really needed it to stay that way.

Next weekend, then, she tapped in. *Shopping. Last of the big spenders.*

Perfect. Love you, baby.

Paige slid her phone into her huge bag with a sigh.

She loved her mum. They'd always been close. They'd had to be. When her dad was home, it felt as if he was biding his time till his next tour. And when he was off overseas playing cricket it was for months at a time. And as it had turned out most of that time was spent shacked up with some girl or another while her mum looked the other way...

Paige would never let herself be taken advantage of in that way. Never let someone mean so much it would be to the detriment of her own dreams. Never be made a fool of for love. Not for all the raspberry white-chocolate muffins on the planet.

When she felt the deepening evening crowd parting around her, Paige shoved her hands under her armpits to get the feeling back into them as she walked a little more slowly home.

Her recent malaise really made no sense at all. Her life was perfect because she was in complete control.

And she knew how to prove it.

* * *

Gabe lounged on his huge uncomfortable leather couch; still in his jacket and boots, legs splayed in front, neck resting against the hard back, eyes closed to the cool moonlight spilling over him.

He'd read so many memos, reports, and projections regarding taking BonaVenture public there was no doubt the company was in better shape than he and Nate could ever have dreamed it could be. He should be feeling damn proud. Vindicated. Relieved. Instead he was so restless he could barely sit still.

Gabe reached for his keys, suddenly needing to go... somewhere, anywhere but the big, empty, cold, lifeless room in which he sat. In which his every thought seemed to echo. Tracking down the one thing that seemed to quiet those thoughts seemed as good a place to start as any.

He paused at his front door when he realised he had no idea which apartment number was hers. To hell with it—he'd knock on every door till he found the right one.

He opened his door, the lift dinged, and the doors slid open. And as if he'd conjured her from thin air, there Paige stood, soft and pink-cheeked, her blonde hair gathered off her face in a wind-tousled knot.

He opened his mouth to joke about the errant lift being his new best friend for having brought her to him again, but at the slow lift and fall of her chest, the quick swipe of her tongue over her plump bottom lip, his throat came over too tight and every muscle in his body was hit with a sudden dull ache.

If he'd had any illusions that the lift *had* brought

her there by accident, they went up in flames the moment Paige lifted her right hand and unfurled a row of condoms. The silver foil wrappers swung from her fingers, glinting at him and sending tracks of fire through his veins.

A growl rose in his throat, and along with it the urge to throw her over his shoulder and drag her back into his cave. But it seemed she had ideas of her own.

She stepped out of the lift, tucked the edge of a condom wrapper between her teeth, and slid a pin from her hair, allowing it to tumble over her shoulders.

She dropped a couple of inches of height as her boots hit the floor with a double *klump klump*. Next came her scarf, uncoiling from around her neck far too slowly before it pooled at her feet. Then, as she watched him from beneath her long lashes, her breaths coming harder again, her fingers moved to the top button of her cardigan. Gabe had to dig his toes into his shoes until they hurt in order to stand still, knowing he'd never forgive himself if he didn't let this play itself out.

The long strip of silver foil still dangled from her teeth as she padded his way, and slowly, achingly slowly, undid each button until she opened it to reveal beautiful soft skin and a pale pink lace bra, the dark circles of her nipples drawing his hungry gaze.

As she came level with him she slid the demure cardigan from her shoulders, her breasts pressing forward, her back arching. When she hooked the cardigan on the end of one fine finger and twirled it over her head, at the aroma of her hot skin wafting past his nose his patience finally gave out.

Gabe lifted her off her feet and threw her over his shoulder fireman style and a whoosh of her laughter filled his lofty apartment.

The second he'd seen her all the blood in his body had headed for his groin. The second he touched her he was rock hard, ready. It took every ounce of self-control he possessed to place her down gently. Her stockinged feet landed with a soft touch on his hard floor.

She took the row of condoms from between her teeth, tucked them into the back pocket of his jeans, her hands lingering on his backside a moment. He gritted his teeth to keep from exploding on the spot as her soft hands moved up his torso to press his jacket aside. She shoved it down his arms and to the floor, and then she was on her toes, her hands beneath his T-shirt, his muscles clenching at the firm touch of her determined fingers.

And then her mouth was on his. Hot, lush, bliss. He wrapped his arms around her and lifted her bodily off the floor to feel her body against the length of his. All he could think was so hot, so soft, so beautiful. The urge to get her horizontal was getting harder to push back, when he remembered belatedly that he *still* didn't have a bed.

Irrelevant. His apartment might be stark, but his imagination was not.

He backed her into the pool of light by the kitchen, needing to see her, to live through her every reaction. Her breath hitched as he bunched her skirt in his big hands, only to come in contact with a hard man's worst nightmare. Tights. He glanced down. Dark pink, they were, like the colour of her skin when she blushed.

Hell. Was she trying to kill him? When she started to shimmy her skirt down, her body rubbing against his, he was sure of it.

He thanked everything that was good and holy that the tights were going south as well. Like a man in trouble, he sank to his knees to worship those legs. Drinking in the tiny V of her G-string, her pale thighs. His hands were so dark against her pale skin as he circled her lean calves, traced her fine ankles, spent extra time on the soft spot behind her knee when he saw it made her shake.

When her fingers slid into his hair, hard and reckless, he placed a single kiss at the juncture of her thighs, marking his place, before he kissed his way up her beautiful body. The curve of her stomach, the dip of her navel, the jut of her hip, the shadow of her breasts and back to her mouth, hot, ready, waiting. The gates of heaven.

When he lifted her and plonked her on the kitchen bench, she cried out and flinched as her warm bottom met the cold granite. He swallowed her gasp, and it turned into a groan. Her lovely long legs hooked around his waist, pulling him to her with an urgency he understood.

When the heat at her centre bore against him and his tether ran out.

Pants off. Condom on. He hooked her underwear to one side and nudged the head of his penis against her centre. The swift intake of breath as he stretched her killed him just a little more.

His eyes met hers to find them wide. But hungry. Her nostrils flared with every intake of breath and her cheeks were so pink with desire he couldn't stand it any longer. He plunged into her. She cried out, pleasure and shock twisting on her face before she tilted her hips to take him deeper, tighter.

If he'd thought her mouth the gates of heaven, deep inside her was heaven itself. So hot, and tight, her muscles clenching around him as together they found a perfect rhythm.

He opened his eyes to find hers on his. Like twin blue flames, hypnotic, drawing him in until he felt the ache build deep inside. He needed every last effort to hold back, even as he rocked into her, deeper, harder. He stopped breathing altogether when her mouth dropped open, her eyes turned to liquid, her breaths to short sharp gasps, and her fingers to talons in his back as she came. Then, after a moment of the most gripping stillness, his world crashed around him in waves of hot, hard, liquid heat.

He came to and found her shaking in his arms. The chill of unheated air touched his skin, turning his sweat to ice. He lifted her off the bench, wrapping his long arms around her until their combined body heat warmed them both.

Her eyes caught his and he took her in. The cool blonde exterior. The wild heat pulsing so close to the surface. Just what he needed. For now.

He opened his mouth to say...who knew what? But she silenced him with a kiss. Soft, sensual and steadying.

Then with a light scrape of fingernails across the stubble of his cheeks, she moved away, stepped into her skirt. Padded through his still-open front door to find her clothes, putting them back on as she went before twisting her long, dishevelled hair back into a makeshift knot.

And then she was in the lift and gone, leaving him with his pants still around his ankles.

'Dear God,' Gabe said, running his hands over his face. That had been hot. Scorching. And they hadn't said a single word to one another the entire time.

He pulled up his jeans, leaving the fly undone, and leant his weary self against the kitchen bench, imagining her in the lift, skin pink from ravishing, clothes rumpled, lips swollen, pretty blue eyes as dark as night. And impossibly he found himself getting hard for her again.

Gabe pushed himself away from the bench, and padded into his bedroom on the way to his shower. He nearly tripped over his laptop bag, which had remained unopened since he'd walked in the door. In fact it had remained unopened all day.

He couldn't remember a day in the past several years he hadn't spent glued to the thing, searching out the next big idea. Collating, researching, and filling his head with every nuance of it so that he would not fail to land it. His gran had raised him to work hard, and make her proud. And since the time he'd failed her so spectacularly on the latter, he'd redoubled his efforts at the former. And while he'd never quite managed to regain that flicker of brilliance he'd felt the night BonaVenture was born, he'd never seen failure since.

But rather than feeling antsy at not working himself to exhaustion, he felt smug as hell. BonaVenture was so healthy it was radiant. And he'd had himself some mind-blowing sex with a beautiful woman who seemed so in tune with his preference to have a good time and not push for anything more, finding her was nothing short of serendipitous.

If he didn't let himself enjoy the spoils of his labour every now and then, what the hell was the point?

As Paige waited in the foyer for the lift the next afternoon, she was still in a bit of a daze, wondering where she'd found it inside her to head to a man's apartment, strip for him, have her way with him, then leave.

She'd never done anything like that before, but she liked it. After years of being so categorically careful, a little recklessness was a revelation. Even a relief. The world seemed that bit brighter, colours richer, the spring in her step springier. She'd even had an even more awesome day at work. Probably something to do with great sex being good for the blood vessels or some such thing.

Maybe she should indulge in a fling every now and then from now on; find some stranger to give her life the occasional splash of panache. Airports could be the new bar. Find someone looking lost and lonely and bam! Her next date.

She was laughing out loud when the lift doors opened, but all her confidence turned to mush when she got in the lift that afternoon to find Gabe already on board, lounging resplendently in the back corner. His dark eyes connected with hers, lit, burned, and it was all she could do to keep blushing from head to toe.

Funny, because now they were even, or nearabouts.

Though perhaps she still owed him an orgasm. She stepped inside the lift, feeling his dark eyes on her, and thought it seemed as good a time as any to remind him as much—

'Good afternoon, Ms Danforth,' a female voice said.

And Paige leapt fair out of her skin. Her gaze jumped sideways to find Mrs Addable from the ninth floor tucked into the front corner, stroking Randy, her Russian Blue whose hair was the same solid dark grey as his owner's.

'Mrs Addable, hi,' Paige mumbled as she slipped into the gap, behind Mrs Addable, and beside Gabe, who looked straight ahead even while his body heat reached out to her like an invitation. 'Randy okay?'

Mrs Addable rolled her eyes. 'He's decided he's too good for his litter tray. We now have to take a constitutional down to the garden near the parking lot four times a day.'

Mrs Addable's eyes slid over lounging Gabe to Paige, who was standing as still and upright as a tower. The older woman's sharp eyes softened to a dull gleam.

'You're Gabe Hamilton,' Mrs Addable said.

'That I am,' Gabe's deep voice rang out.

Paige had to swallow hard so as not to tremble as the sound reverberated deliciously through her bones. She remembered all too well the feel of his breath against her cheek that came with the exquisite sensation of having him inside her.

'Gloria Addable. 9B. I heard Sam the Super talking to Mr Klempt the other day about your arrival.'

'Pleasure to meet you, Gloria.'

'Likewise, Gabe.'

No *Mr Hamilton*, Paige noticed. She'd lived in the building for two years and had yet to progress from polite surnames from anyone in that apartment bar the cat.

'Sam said you'd had some trouble with your bed?' Mrs Addable added, eyes now front, watching the movement of floor numbers, the slow strokes to Randy's back causing the cat to purr.

'True, yet I've managed remarkably well,' he said, pulling himself upright, bringing him closer.

Paige looked directly ahead, not daring to meet his eyes. Yet she felt a beat pulse between them. Two. Three.

'I have a spare mattress I can send up,' Mrs Addable tried again. 'It's only a single, but...'

While Mrs Addable droned on about the history of her single mattress, Paige felt Gabe move closer still. Close enough when she breathed the sleeve of his jacket brushed against the sleeve of hers.

Then he said, 'My bed arrived this morning.'

Forgetting propriety completely, Paige shot her gaze straight to his. 'It did?'

Mrs Addable's snort of triumph barely touched the edges of her sub-conscious. Gabe's dark and dangerous eyes had a funny way of blocking out everything else.

His voice was low as he said, 'The service lift, it seems, is less touchy.'

'That's great,' Paige said, adding a belated, 'For *you*.'

Gabe's cheek lifted in the beginnings of the kind of smile that meant big trouble for her. 'I'm glad—for me—too.'

The lift binged and when Paige and Mrs Addable

both turned with expectation towards the doors, Gabe took the chance to slide his finger down the edge of Paige's. The shock of his touch shot through her like a bushfire, spreading in half a second flat to the whole of her chest and the ends of her curling toes.

The door opened to the fourth floor. Where nobody was waiting. And stayed there.

Mrs Addable sighed. 'It's okay, Randy. We'll get there eventually.'

As the lift went up and down the next ten minutes, Paige locked her knees, and bit her bottom lip, and prayed for the strength not to moan out loud as Gabe's thumb traced circles over the wildly fluctuating pulse at her wrist, making her so woozy she saw spots.

And for the first time since she'd moved into the building she was thankful she had a Machiavellian lift.

FIVE

It took more than fifteen stupid minutes for the stupid lift to open at Paige's floor on the night of Gabe's party. Way too much time in which to wonder if she ought to change her dress. Her hair. Her mind.

She felt edgy. Hyper-aware. As if she could feel even the slightest shift of air dancing across her skin. Because after several days of living out the most hot, illicit, exciting affair of her life under cover of darkness in the privacy of Gabe's moon-drenched loft, the real world was about to impose on their heretofore perfect little bubble of secret sex.

The lift doors began to close and she slipped inside at the last second, squeezing into a gap amongst a group of bright shiny young things, none of whom she'd ever met. Why would she have? She and Gabe knew hardly anything about one another outside the bedroom.

Which was fine. Perfect really. It kept things super casual.

She wished she'd brought up the party once, at least to get a gauge of what she might be about to walk into. Would she and Gabe treat one another as virtual strangers? As friendly neighbours? Or would they simply avoid one another all night?

This, she thought. *This* was why she liked things to be simple, straightforward, with all the cards on the table from the very beginning. This nervous tumbling in her stomach was awful. And horribly familiar. Surely it was a symptom that something wasn't right.

As the lift rose the deep *whump whump whump* of music pulsed in her bones, lifting the energy throbbing deep within her to screaming point. The lift opened, and the sounds of party chatter and, ironically, Billy Idol singing 'Hot in the City' spilled into the lift as the inhabitants tumbled out.

Paige took a deep breath, smoothed a hand over her new dress, ran another over her hair, then with chin tilted she walked into Gabe's penthouse.

As it turned out, Paige knew plenty of people. Mrs Addable and several other inhabitants of the building huddled by the windows checking out the view. She saw a few girls from uni, and even a couple of guys she'd dated. She felt an odd surge of disappointment. She shook it off. She wasn't special to Gabe and she didn't want to be.

She nearly managed to convince herself as much when a quick glance around the jam-packed room revealed a massive red and grey rug now covering the lounge-room floor. A large red urn bursting with a tall spray of stripped willow. And chairs and tables in every place they ought to be. A half second after she got over the surprise of Gabe having *decorated* she realised every item was from that season's Ménage à Moi catalogue. The bubbles in her stomach went haywire.

Then the hairs on the back of her neck began to prickle, as though she was being watched. In a party that size someone somewhere would be smouldering at someone, and it was likely she'd been caught in the crossfire. And yet…

Rolling her shoulders to fend off the scratchy sensation, she turned, eyes searching the crowd until they landed on a pair of familiar dark eyes.

Gabe stood on the far side of the large room, his back to the floor-to-ceiling windows, a near full moon and a million stars twinkling in the inky black sky his backdrop. He was so deliciously handsome, so unsettling, so *much*. And his eyes were focused entirely on her. Dark eyes of a man who was near addicted to doughnuts, knew more about Doris Day movies than she did, and who remembered where she worked even though she was sure she hadn't mentioned it since the day they first met.

She liked that he was leaving. Liked that he was discreet. Liked that every time she saw him he could barely keep his hands off her. But the riot of sensation ripping through her in that moment was so beyond mere *like* she hadn't a hope of naming it.

She clutched her silver lamé purse in one hand, and the small box she'd brought with her, so hard they left imprints on her palms.

'Paige!' Mae's voice rang sharp in her ear.

Paige blinked, the noise and energy and light and

life of the party rushing in on her as if she'd burst from a tunnel. Then the crowd shifted, and Gabe was gone.

Paige turned to find Mae shoving through the crowd and bundling up to her like a ball of energy, Clint lolloping in her wake.

'How cool is this?' asked Mae. 'And my godfather, this apartment! You must be dying to get stuck into it.'

Paige opened her mouth to tell Mae this was Gabe's version of decorated, until she remembered that according to Mae this was the first time Paige had been there too. She hadn't meant to keep the thing with Gabe from Mae, but they'd barely seen one another in the past week, and she'd been so busy at work— And it had been so intense, so unlike anything she'd ever done before, she hadn't wanted the bubble to burst.

She'd fill Mae in on all the juicy details the first moment they had some girly time together, just the two of them. She glanced across at the ever-present Clint and wondered when that might be.

'Where is that delicious pirate of yours?' Mae asked. 'The guy was clearly into you at The Brasserie last week, and he looks like the kind of guy who doesn't need a flashlight and a map to find your treasure, if ya know what I mean.'

Paige rolled her eyes even while she knew it to be the absolute truth. Gabe Hamilton had found her treasure no problem at all. In fact, her treasure was so attuned to him she was doing her best to ignore the heavy ache in her treasure just thinking about him.

'Drinks!' Mae said and Clint looked as if he was reminded again why he wanted to marry her. Then hand in hand they made a beeline for the bar.

Leaving Paige to pretend every fibre of her being wasn't paying intense heed to their host, wherever he might be.

Gabe ran a finger beneath the V of his sweater for about the hundredth time since a bunch of strangers had piled into his apartment.

He'd be pushing it to say he knew even a tenth of them, and a half of *those* he'd met in the lift at one point or another that week. The rest were a blur of hair and teeth that Nate had introduced to him, talking each and every one up as though they were the next big thing. He got it, Nate was trying to make him feel at home. Yet the only thing keeping him from making a hasty exit in search of fresh air, no matter how cold, had been brief glimpses of a familiar head of cool-blonde hair.

He'd known the moment Paige had arrived—some shift in the air, some call of the wild to his hormones had him sniffing the air for her scent. And then she'd appeared through the crowd in a white dress that looked as if she'd been poured into it and revealed enough leg to give a less vital man palpitations.

His gaze found her again, this time talking to some guy. Her hair shifting across her back as she talked. When the guy moved in, placing a hand on her upper arm, waving his big watch in her face, something clenched hot and hard deep inside Gabe. Something primal and not pretty.

'It's the legs,' said a voice cutting into his thoughts.

He turned to find a group of men in sharp suits

standing beside him, all cradling half-filled glasses, all looking in Paige's direction.

'What's that?' asked Gabe.

'They're like something out of a forties detective movie,' said another of the men. 'I've spent more time than I dare admit imagining myself as Sam Spade, walking into a smoke-filled room, sunlight pouring through slatted blinds, to find those legs crossed as she sits waiting on my desk.'

'Hamilton, right?' asked the third. 'We're friends of Nate's.'

'Right,' said Gabe, brushing off the fact that Nate seemed to have more friends he didn't know than friends he did. There were more pressing matters. 'You know Paige?'

At the dark tone of his voice three pairs of male eyes turned his way. Turned, and softened. He could all but hear them thinking, *Poor mug, thinks he's in with a chance.*

Never in his life had Gabe felt a stronger urge to kiss and tell. *I've had her up against a wall, on the kitchen bench, crying out my name so loud the whole damn building must have heard.* But he lifted his glass and filled his mouth with Scotch before his foot landed there instead.

'Dated her one time,' said the first, 'before she introduced me to my wife.'

'Cool move,' said the second with a laugh.

'Cool creature,' said the third.

Gabe's gaze drew back to Paige. He caught her profile as she smiled and waved at someone across the room. Her smile was calm. Understated. He could see why people might think her cool, he'd thought so himself at one point, but now he understood it was a mask, a mode of self-protection. Something tickled the back of his mind, as if he were trying to catch the disparate threads of a dream.

Familiarity, perhaps. Maybe even a recognition of his own natural reserve.

Or déjà vu.

Another cool blonde of his acquaintance came crashing into his mind, right along with the tightness in his gut as he'd first spied that long ago blonde smiling at him from across the room at BonaVenture's first big party, and the smile that never quite reached her eyes unless they met his.

'No,' he said, out loud, turning heads. Grimacing, he downed the last of his Scotch before slamming the glass onto a passing tray.

This wasn't the same as that. For one thing he'd been young, and cocky, and ruled by his libido. He was older, wiser now and kept that part of him on a short leash. And yet his subconscious wouldn't let it lie. This thing with Paige was...intense. And it had ignited exceptionally fast. Who could blame him? The woman was so lush and lovely she kept him half hard half the day and all the way all night.

He ground a thumb and forefinger into his eyes, but the memories continued to knock against the inside of his brain.

He'd met Lydia right as BonaVenture had hit the crest of its first wave of success. The business that had been a mere dream a few years before had gone stratospheric right after his gran had died. And it was as though he'd gone to sleep one night himself, and woken up to find the world as he'd always known it was simply no more.

Lydia had been his port in the storm, and it had never occurred to him that her motivations in being with him might have been anything less than romantic. In the end that error of judgement had all but destroyed everything he and Nate had worked so hard to build.

And here he was, set to make the biggest financial decision of his life, and he'd gone and entangled himself in a blonde distraction once again.

'Having fun?' Nate said, slapping Gabe on the back, rocking him back on his heels.

A dark cloud hovering about his ears, Gabe shoved his fingers hard into the front pockets of his jeans. 'So much so I barely know how to contain myself.'

Nate snorted. 'Now quickly, I have a thing in Sydney this week. A meet and greet with an upstart encryption software company. Looks schmick. I was going to send Rick, but I'm not sure that he's as net savvy as—Gabe?'

'Hmm?' A sliver of white glinting through the crowd had snagged Gabe's attention. 'What now?'

'I was being about as subtle as a woman in red lipstick. I'm offering you a lifeline, mate. An actual prospective client to sound out while you're here. Thought you'd jump at the chance to sink your fangs into an actual real live deal.'

Normally he would, but he was in a questioning type of mood, and even while Nate's face was a picture of innocence, so far everything he'd said or done that night had screamed ulterior motive.

'Unless you have other plans? More decorating perhaps? Like what you've done with the place so far. Very...pretty.'

Gabe cut him a glower. 'Considering your flair for interior design I take that as a compliment. When's the flight?'

'Daybreak tomorrow. And you're welcome.'

Gabe caught the glint of light on blonde hair move through the swarm and heard himself say, 'Make it a day later and I'm there.'

He felt Nate's incredulous stare. Pretended he didn't.

Nate said, 'Am I missing something here? I've had people manning the lifts at work in case you slipped out and were never heard from again— Ri-i-ight. I see.' Nate grabbed a tiny pastry from a passing tray and threw it into his mouth. 'So who's the blonde?'

Gabe breathed out long and slow. He'd been quietly concerned about the ever-decreasing degrees of separation between Paige and Nate and confirmation that Nate wasn't a paid-up member of the 'I Fantasise About Paige's Legs' club was more of a relief than he cared to admit. Gabe set his vision at the middle distance, and drawled, 'Any blonde in particular you need me to soften up for you?'

Nate grabbed him by the ears and turned his head the half-inch to face the blonde in question. 'The one who has you dancing about like you have ants in your pants. The one making you think twice about getting out of bed early tomorrow.'

Gabe swiped his hands away. 'For starters, I don't dance. And secondly she lives in the building and...' She what? Wasn't the reason why he was actually considering shucking off work? The dark cloud surrounded his whole head. 'She all but shut the lift doors on my fingers when we first met.'

'That's it? Well, then you won't mind if I head that way and—'

Gabe's hand shot out and grabbed Nate by the back of the neck.

Nate laughed as he ducked out of Gabe's grip. 'Been so long since I've seen you even look twice at a blonde, it's bloody reassuring. Like you're really back. Not just here, but *back*. Now, seems I have to go tell poor Rick he has an early start in the morning.'

With that, Nate headed off, leaving Gabe silenced. And shrouded in more grey clouds than ever. Of all times for Nate to slant a reference at Lydia... He'd dated blondes since her, surely? Lydia hadn't screwed him over *that* much.

Sure she'd sold their pillow talk with the competition, leading to an investigation by the Australian Securities Commission for insider trading, which had meant the near undoing of the business into which he and Nate had poured their hearts and souls, the repercussions of which had sent him careening off to all four corners of the globe in an effort to wrench Bona-Venture from the grips of obliteration—

But it wasn't as if it affected him any more. Unless you counted the fact that he was more vigilant when it came to his business dealings. Perhaps even a little zealously so. But his dating habits were peachy. Or at least they would be once all the monkeys finally left his apartment.

All bar one.

Paige sensed Gabe a good second before his deep dark voice said, 'Miss Danforth, how good of you to come.'

She took a quick heartening gulp from her champagne, then turned and said, 'Why, of course.' At least she planned to. But nothing came out.

In leather and a three-day growth Gabe Hamilton looked like a sexy pirate. In pyjama bottoms and nothing else he was every woman's fantasy. In a cool pinstriped jacket, navy cashmere sweater, and dark jeans he looked so delectably tactile he was more dangerous than ever.

When he leant to place a soft warm kiss on her cheek she had a fair idea of what oxygen deprivation must feel like—all breathless and weak and woozy, with a touch of delirium thrown in.

'For you,' she said, shoving the small box between them. 'Housewarming present.'

He took the package, his brow furrowing as he stared at it. And suddenly she felt silly for bringing anything at all.

She flapped her hand at him. 'On second thoughts, give it back. It so won't go with your gorgeous new decor.'

Pulling the gift out of her reach, he glanced up under his thick dark lashes. 'You noticed.'

'I'd be pretty sucky at my job if I didn't. It looks great. You did good.'

He cocked his head in thanks. Then brought her gift to his ear and gave it a little shake. 'So long as it's not a throw cushion I'm sure it'll do fine.'

All she could do was shrug, while she felt more and more sure that what was meant to be a funny little trinket was too ridiculous, too overfamiliar, too obvious he'd made an impact on her. But then she thought of the big changes he'd made to his apartment, because of her, and didn't quite know what to think any more.

He opened the box, a wash of surprise, bewilderment, and laughter playing over his beautiful face as he stared at the hot-pink flamingo in his big dark hands.

'For your phone,' she explained, sliding her hand to the inside pocket of his jacket, knowing that was where his ever-present phone would be. She drew it out and placed it neatly into place in the crook of the bird's bent leg. Tilting her head for him to follow, she slipped through a gap in the crowd to put the phone holder on the kitchen bench.

She turned and, with a ta-da move, said, 'To keep the doughnut crumbs away.'

Gabe blinked at the kitsch splash of pink adorning his sleek dark kitchen, then back to her. His silky dark eyes looking *right* into her. She knew how Lois Lane felt knowing Superman's X-ray vision meant he could tell what colour undies she wore. She felt the same desire to hide behind something big and solid for protection.

Waving her hand in front of her dramatically pinking face, she said, 'It's a silly little—'

'It's perfect,' he said, placing a hand over his heart. 'Thank you.'

'My pleasure.' And it was. *He* was. Her complete and

utter pleasure. A pleasure she'd actually thought might fizzle in the glaring light of a public outing.

The crowd jostled and she bumped against him. He gathered her with a strong arm until she was flush against his big strong front, the heat of him bleeding through her barely there dress. Again she wondered how she'd gone so long without a man in her life. Without the mouth-watering ache inside her. How? Because it had never felt like this before.

'Let's get the hell out of here,' Gabe's voice rumbled through her.

Paige laughed. 'But the party's just started.'

'Really? Feels like it's been going on for days.'

When it began to dawn on her he might not be kidding, she glanced over his shoulder at the party going great guns behind him. 'But don't you need to—?'

'Not so much.'

Her eyes swung back to his to find them drenched with desire. For her. The hot ache sank and spread until she would have collapsed in a quivering puddle of pure need had Gabe not been holding her.

When the urge to grab his hand and run, dispatching a coat-hanger tackle on anyone in her path, swelled hot and fast inside her, Paige knew then that she'd gone past the point of curing her dating-drought.

She'd cracked.

Relinquishing a degree of control had seemed a worthy price to pay to find her feet again. But the raging desire to give in and do whatever Gabe asked of her was so strong it scared her. It felt like a heck of a short trip from that to becoming her mother, watching the clock, marking off the calendar, blushing hopefully every time the phone rang. And living a life of perpetual disappointment.

She locked her knees and pressed her hands into his chest, steadfastly ignoring the urge to curl her fingernails against the hard planes. 'Gabe, you have to stay.'

He slowly shook his head. 'I have to have you.'

Good God. Paige licked her lips, preparing to explain why he'd have to wait but there were simply no words. She bit her bottom lip to stop from whimpering. His dark gaze honed in on the movement, a muscle jumping in his cheek. The hastening of his heartbeat beneath her palms was her undoing.

'Okay. Let's go,' she said.

Apparently that was all Gabe needed. He grabbed her hand and drew her through the crowd, parting it like a hot knife through butter.

'Gabe!' a voice broke into her buzzing sub-conscious.

Fully expecting Gabe to accelerate into a sprint, Paige was so surprised when he actually stopped she banged into his back, and had to grip his arm in order to steady herself. He wrapped his arm around her in order to steady her, so she was all wrapped up in him when she found herself the subject of some shrewd attention from a man she'd never met.

'Now what?' Gabe said, his impatience clear as day.

The party guest, handsome in a clean-cut jock kind of way, smiled patiently at Gabe, and then at her.

Gabe sighed, then said, 'Nate Mackenzie, Paige Danforth.'

Nate grinned as he held out a hand. 'The infamous lift monopolist. Pleasure.'

Paige laughed in surprise. Then glanced at Gabe to

find him quietly fuming at his friend. A friend he'd talked to about her. While she'd never said a word to Mae. Mae who was somewhere at the party, clueless she was about to do a bunk. Her stomach clutched more than a little.

'One last thing before you depart,' Nate said to Gabe. 'The men in grey by the window. Go say "hi".'

Gabe growled so low Paige winced. 'Another time.'

Paige felt Nate's attention focus on her even as he held Gabe's dark gaze with his deceptively smiling eyes. 'This is the only time. We need them. For the... deal.'

Gabe's grip tightened on hers and she prepared to make a dash for the door. But when her eye slid to his it was to see a muscle clenching in his cheek.

To her he'd always seemed basically untouchable. As if nothing could topple him. In that moment he looked like a fish on a hook. A fish who could have thrown the hook with little more than a jerk of his great head if he'd decided to do so. But a fish who was currently chewing on the hook instead, gritting it between his teeth, before he squared his shoulders, apologised to her for a momentary change of plans, and took off.

'Sorry,' Nate said, clearly meaning it. 'Business, you know.'

'That's fine,' she said, even though she hadn't a clue. She barely knew what Gabe did for a living. It involved travel, a phone that might as well be permanently attached to his hand, and...men in suits, apparently.

'I'm his partner at BonaVenture,' Nate said. 'And by the look in your eyes he's never mentioned me to you.'

'Sorry.'

They'd never talked that much about her work either. Which added to growing worry gnawing at her innards, because her work was pretty much the most significant thing in her life. Only the past week that distinction had been usurped by the man standing stiff-backed amongst a group of men who were grinning and fawning, shaking his hand as if he were some kind of rock star.

'If only he wasn't one of a kind.'

'Hmm?'

Nate ran a hard hand up the back of his neck, eyes zeroed in on the conversation on the other side of the room. 'Gabe. He's brilliant, you know.'

She didn't know that either, actually. Oh, she knew the man had skills, but she was fairly sure she and Nate were thinking of quite different ones.

'I have a good line in spin,' Nate continued, 'but Gabe? He's a superstar. He can smell potential from a continent away. He can seduce even the most timid ideas men to let him in. Nobody else out there like him. My life would be a hell of a lot simpler if there were.'

Nate's astute gaze slewed from Gabe and back to her, his mouth lifting into a smile so self-confident it completely belied his previous words. She could see in that look why the two men got along. They were both forces of nature. And even while she had no idea what was going on behind Nate's clever hazel eyes it gave her goose bumps.

Then Nate said, 'If you have any kind of influence over him—'

She held up her hands and waved them frantically

enough to stop Nate in his tracks. 'I don't. Honestly. We're...friends.'

For a perfectly nice term, 'friends' sounded such a lame description for what they were, and Nate's raised eyebrows told her he wasn't buying it either.

But he backed down. 'Apologies. Clearly I'm getting desperate.'

'For?'

'Him to stay, of course.'

The worries that had been little fissures splintered to form the Grand Canyon. 'He's *considering* sticking around?'

'You tell me.'

She swallowed past the tightness in her throat. Like a good many things, they hadn't talked about when he was leaving as an actual couple would, because they weren't an actual couple. They were...flinging. And to protect herself from any damage the act of flinging might incur, she'd done a lot of assuming. And you knew what they said about assuming?

She *needed* him to go. The only reason she was taking chances where she'd never taken them before was because it had an end date.

As if he knew she was thinking about him, Gabe looked back across the room. As their eyes connected she could practically see the energy arcing between them.

Gabe shook his head once, promising he wouldn't be long. Or was he saying, *Don't get any ideas, now. Don't make the mistake of falling for me*? On any other man the warning would be conceited. Gabe ought to have had it tattooed on his bicep at birth.

It seemed she'd been right to try to protect herself from fling damage. Only problem was, it hadn't worked.

SIX

—

The sound of the party spilled through the closed front doors of Gabe's apartment as Paige pressed the lift button, her finger shaking, whether from anticipation of what was to come or aftermath of the conversation with Nate. Probably a mixture of both.

She glanced up, and caught Gabe's eye. Remembered the warmth that had flooded her the night she'd caught him smiling at her over a doughnut while he leant against his kitchen bench in unbuttoned jeans and felt a tiny stab of fear that Mae wasn't the only one she was hiding things from any more. So she blurted, 'When are you going back to Brazil?'

'I'm not,' he said, and Paige's stomach fell to her shoes. Then, 'That deal's done. But I will be leaving as soon as I'm done here. I follow the work, and ninety per cent of the time it's many *many* miles from here.'

She breathed out a sigh of relief so loud she closed her eyes tight against the embarrassment of it.

When she finally lifted her head it was to find his eyes were closed. His lips parted as he found his natural breath. The bright lights of the lift created shadows beneath his brows, highlighting every crinkle around his eyes, every hair on his jaw, the curve of his Adam's apple.

He was so much man it made her chest hurt just looking at him.

He opened his eyes, gave her a small smile, tucked a stray lock of hair behind her ear, and then his eyes left hers to drift over her face. Hovering momentarily on her hair, her neck, her lips.

This, she thought, swallowing hard.

Raging attraction plus wedding-dress-purchase-recoil had sent her into his arms in the first place but *this* was why she wasn't yet ready to walk away. The way she felt when they were alone together. Work, family, Mae; they didn't come up because they didn't matter. He stilled her mind. Made everything feel simple. Let her live in the moment.

She reached up and traced the backs of her knuckles along the hollow of his cheek. Ran a thumb softly over his bottom lip. Smoothed a stray hair in his eyebrow. And he let her. His eyes gave nothing away, but his nostrils flared at her quiet touch.

When the feeling inside her began to swell so large she struggled to find a full breath Paige curled her fingers into her palm and pressed herself against the wall so that they could disentangle themselves. Gabe fixed his pants, she fixed her dress, both of them flickering sly glances at each other, before they both burst out laughing.

'You, Miss Danforth, are a revelation,' he said.

'Would you believe before you came along I was a bit of a good girl?'

His dark eyes connected long and hard with hers for long enough that her breath caught in her throat. Then, as he reached for the emergency button, he said, 'Nah.'

And Paige laughed again, light, free. Happy. Even as she revelled in the feeling, she knew it was dangerous.

Gabe didn't notice as he was jabbing and jiggling the emergency button. Yet the lift refused to budge.

Giving her dress a last fix, she joined him. 'You're kidding me, right?'

Gabe spared her a flat glance, before reaching into his jacket pocket for his mobile to call for help. Only to find it was missing.

'The flamingo,' they said as one, and Paige laughed so hard she clutched her stomach.

'This isn't funny. There are over a hundred people stuck up there.'

'And it'll only take one to leave early to notice the lift's not working.' Paige put a finger to her bottom lip. 'If not for the fact that the lift is a total diva at the best of times.'

A muscle jumped in Gabe's cheek and she realised he was beginning to look kind of stressed. Poor love.

'Here,' she said, pressing him aside to pop the hatch to find the lift's emergency phone. It was busted. Seriously, at the next tenants' meeting she was bringing out a whole bag of whoop on Sam the Super's ass.

Gabe ran a hand through his hair as his gaze shot up, down, and at the seam in the lift's doors.

And something occurred to Paige. 'Gabe. Are you claustrophobic?'

He tugged at the V of his sweater. 'Of course not. But neither am I keen on feeling trapped in a small space for an extended period of time. This rotten, stinking, no good—' Gabe said, his voice now not much more than a growl as he banged at the control panel with enough force to bruise. Still the lift didn't budge.

Paige lost it. Laughing so hard now she hiccuped. 'See!' she managed to get out. 'It's not just me. This is fantastic. And I was so sure he'd fallen under your spell.'

'He?'

Paige blinked up at Gabe, whose eyes were narrowed dangerously in her direction. She was the one who'd hit the button in the first place after all.

Her bottom lip slid straight between her teeth and his gaze slid straight to her mouth, his eyes darkening, his breath lengthening, as she said, 'Rock Hudson, of course.'

Then his eyes shot back to hers, and the corner of his mouth lifted in a dangerous smile.

Silence stretched between them, only broken by the occasional creak of the lift. They were left with nothing to do but wait.

'So,' Paige said, crossing her arms, cocking her hip, 'what now?'

'What kind of name is Gabe?'

Gabe's thighs burned from being on his haunches the past ten minutes as he tried to rewire the phone and get them the hell out of the box. He could sniff out creative accounting in a company report from a mile away, but he knew less than nothing about electrical engineering.

'Just Gabe? Or short for Gabriel?' Paige added when it became clear he wasn't about to answer.

'Short,' he said.

'That's sweet,' she said, clearly not as concerned as he was about the thinning of the air. 'Like the angel.'

Gabe's knees creaked as he pulled himself to standing. He turned to find Paige standing in the far corner of the lift, one bare foot on top of the other, her hair now up in a makeshift knot, the ends of his sports coat rolled up at her wrists. Despite the stale air all sorts of parts of him stirred for her again. He shot them down. He was conserving air. 'You having fun over there while I try to get us out of here?'

'Tonnes. I'm used to being the one swearing under my breath at this thing. It's nice to watch someone else have a turn.'

'Nice ain't the word I'd use.' Gabe looked around the small space. No way was he something so pansy-assed as *claustrophobic*. Though time spent in parts of the world with less than exemplary examples of modern vertical architecture had left him with an ever so slight discordance with elevator travel.

'Now back to your name—'

'It's a family name,' he said, rubbing his fingers across the stiff back of his neck.

'Mother's side? Father's?'

'Aren't you hot?'

Paige blinked her big blue bedroom eyes at him

and wrapped herself tighter in the cosy warmth of his jacket. Then she slowly shook her head.

'The air-con's been turned off,' he said. 'When did that happen?'

'I haven't been paying attention. But we'll be fine here for hours. I read a book about a guy in Brussels who was stuck in a lift for like a week. Lived off detritus he dug up from the carpet. Hugh Jackman was going to play him in the movie.' She seemed to go far away for a second before she snapped back. 'Compared with him we have it pretty good.'

'Hugh Jackman, or the guy in Brussels?' Gabe asked, trying his best not to imagine being stuck in what amounted to a luxury coffin for days. 'Don't answer that. In fact no more talk.'

Her cheek lifted as she held back a smile. He hadn't realised she was a sadist but she was enjoying his discomfort way too much. Proving it, she slid one foot to the wall, cocking a sexy knee in his direction, drawing her tight dress right up her thigh. Then she took a big deep breath before saying, 'So, Nate seems like a good guy. Great hair. And that dimple? Adorable!'

Gabe clenched his teeth so hard he was sure he heard something crack. 'Are you kidding me?'

She blinked several times over. 'I'm sorry, did you want me to stop asking questions about *you*, or to stop talking altogether?'

He raised one telling eyebrow.

She did the same, and began to swing her knee side to side, drawing his gaze to those legs. Legs that could make a grown man get on his knees and thank God he'd been born. She asked, 'Is Nate single?'

'My father's,' Gabe ground out.

She cupped a hand to her ear. 'I'm sorry?'

'My name comes from my father's side.' He checked the ceiling, wondering at what point he should kick out a panel, climb onto the roof, and shimmy up the metal cord—

'He was a Gabriel?'

Gabe shook his head. 'Frank.'

'*His* father, then?' Paige pressed. 'No? His father's best friend's war buddy's pet llama?'

And whether it was the fact that she was apparently willing to suffocate them both before giving up, or the way she looked so soft and smudged in her pretty bare feet and his big jacket, Gabe gave up something he'd never even shared with Nate. 'My father's mother was a Gabriella.'

It was a small confidence, but the surrendering of it was felt. He was more than surprised when places inside him seemed to shift to accommodate the new-found space.

Paige's knee stopped mid-swing and her bottom lip tucked between her teeth, probably to stop herself from grinning at his namesake, but he didn't much care. The sheen her teeth left in their wake brought on a blood rush of attraction with a vengeance. Screw it. If he was going to die here, he might as well die smiling. Eyes locked onto her mouth, he ambled her way.

She asked, 'This was the grandmother who made sure your Doris Day knowledge was up to snuff?'

'Amongst other things. Gabriel had come through several generations, and Gran had no brothers, so...'

'So not a girlie name, then.'

'Not.' He lifted his eyes to hers, to find them darkened. As if she knew exactly what she did to his blood. And his nerves. And the tempo of his breaths. So long as she never realised she had the ability to shake things loose inside him as well.

She shook a lock of hair from her face and the knot tumbled free over one shoulder. 'Well, I think it's... sweet.'

'Do you, now?'

'Sweet as pie. Sweeter than how my name came about.' She laughed, but there was no humour in it. And when she frowned and looked down at her bare toes curling and uncurling against the floor Gabe stopped in his tracks.

He wasn't adept at deep and meaningfuls. In fact they had the tendency to bring him out in hives. But stuck in the lift, their personal space overlapping, it simply felt decent to ask. 'How's that?'

Several beats pulsed between them before she flicked her hair from her eyes again and said, 'Dad was a cricketer. International. Away eighty per cent of the year. Mum figured he'd be away when I was born—which he was. So, in an effort to include him in my birth, she gave him the job of naming me. Carte blanche.'

Her voice was even, but he felt the cool in her as she spoke. Saw the chips of ice in her warm blue eyes. They echoed inside him, banging painfully against the raw edges of the new space there.

'Want to know who I was named after?' Paige's shoulders lifted as she wrapped her arms tighter around herself, and flicked her hair again.

'More than life itself.'

She laughed even as she frowned at herself for doing so, the husky sound washing over his skin like waves of warmth. 'The maid who'd turned down his bed at the hotel when he'd got the phone call.'

God. What a prick. Instinct had Gabe wanting to run his thumb across the vertical lines above her nose. Circumspection had him pressing his feet hard into the floor.

She tucked the wayward lock behind her ear. 'I think Mum had been hoping to rouse some kind of connection in him. Hoping it would encourage him home more. To us.'

'Did it work?'

Her smile remained, only now it was bittersweet. 'Not so much. He cheated any chance he got, and she scrubbed the kitchen till it shone. Until one day she had enough, and asked for a divorce. He had the gall to be shocked. And even while she took him for plenty, he left her broken.' She shook out her shoulders, and scraped her teeth along her tongue as if trying to get rid of a bad taste in her mouth. 'Anyway. Bygones.'

Bygones, Gabe thought. *Things we pretend don't matter any more. But sweeping them under the rug only creates a lump to be tripped over time and again.* He pushed the thought away.

'Do you see him much? Your dad?'

'Never. Mum and I are pretty close, though. She's a good woman, way more forgiving than I could ever be. Yours?'

He should have seen it coming, but he'd been concentrating so hard on Paige the question came out of left field. And he was caught, looking into her big blue bedroom eyes, all liquid, hurting, wanting, patient.

He could practically feel his heart beating in his neck as the words spilled from his lips. 'They died when I was young. My gran raised me.'

'Gran Gabriella,' she said, nodding, even smiling a little, as if the pieces of him slipped into place.

'She was an amazing woman. Tough. Stubborn. Thank God too. I was a wild kid. Impatient. First to climb the tree. Fastest to the top of the hill. She had a choice to either let me go feral or guide me with a firm hand. All of my focus I owe to her.'

'Is she in Melbourne still?'

'She passed several years back. Right about the time my career took off. It broke my heart that she wasn't around to see it.' As he breathed out he felt another shift, this one so significant he could practically feel air swirling inside him in the place where he'd harboured that regret for so long.

Paige's next breath out was long and slow, as if she too was letting things go. He could have kissed her for leaving it there. Hell, he could have kissed her either way. Her hair falling in wisps about her face. Her lips pink from the nibbling.

'Paige—' he said, but that was all that came as he wasn't sure what he wanted to say.

He actually shook his head at the realisation that she'd rendered him speechless. The rainmaker. The silver-tongued seducer of innocent creatives.

No matter the mistakes he'd made in his life, he'd done something right for her to have come into his life at the right moment. This woman who'd looked so relieved earlier when he'd reiterated that he'd be leaving soon, that their affair had a use-by date, even he'd been a little taken aback. Until he'd given himself a swift mental slap.

Paige was warm, sexy, astute, and gorgeous as all get out, but there was a limit to what he could offer. It was a good thing that he'd been forced to remember what a destructive illusion *feeling* for someone could be. He'd remember with even more biting clarity once he was no longer surrounded by air that smelled so thickly of warm, soft, edible, feminine skin.

He stepped forward and placed his hands on her upper arms. Her warmth seeped from the fabric of his too-big jacket into his skin. Her delicious scent curled beneath his nose. Her big blue eyes looked unblinking into his as her chest rose high and fell hard.

Yes, he thought. *That.* The touchy-feely stuff had made him feel unexpectedly raw, but it had nothing on pure and simple sexual hunger.

He placed a hand on the wall above her head, and heat arched through him as her lips parted, soft and moist and practically begging for his kiss.

When she licked her lips, and tilted her head, the *wanting* that swept through him was thick and consuming. Unrelenting. And limitless, filling all the newly shifted places inside him. He closed his eyes on that thought. Gritted his teeth against the insinuation.

Then at the slide of her hand into the back of his hair, the press of her hips to his groin, the sweet shuddering sigh as her breath whispered across his neck, he thought, *Oh, to hell with it—*

Then the lights flickered. And the lift began to move.

* * *

The lift binged, the doors opened, and Paige knew that if she snapped her eyes left she'd see the silver wallpaper of the eighth floor. But she couldn't snap her eyes any which way, not for all the coffee in Brazil.

Not with Gabe looking at her that way. As if he was looking not at her, but into the very heart of her. She wondered what he saw. If it was a disappointment, all cold and uninviting. Or if it flickered with any of the heat freefalling through her body. If he had any inkling any warmth glowing inside her had been put there by him. She looked away then, and hoped she hadn't left it too late.

'We should probably get out of here before the thing changes it mind,' she said. 'You're way too big for me to carry out of here if your claustrophobia gets the better of you.'

'Funny woman,' said Gabe, though it was apparently enough to get him to move, as he grabbed a door and ushered her through. Without all that concentrated heat burning a hole right through her, Paige somehow managed to put one foot in front of the other to scoop up her heels and purse and exit the lift.

The recessed lighting made the hallway overly bright to Paige's eyes, as if she'd spent a year in a cave, not an hour in a perfectly well-lit lift. As if the confidences she and Gabe had shared had all been a crazy dream. She shucked his jacket from her back and held it out to him on the end of a finger. He took it and tucked it over his crooked elbow.

He angled his head towards the ceiling. 'I'd better

head back up, check everyone's okay. Make sure Nate hasn't invited everyone to sleep over.'

'You're braver than I am.'

'You kidding? I'm taking the stairs. You?'

She wrapped her arms about herself, missing Gabe's jacket, missing his nearness. It was enough to have her take a step back as she shook her head. 'I think I've tempted fate enough tonight.'

His mouth lifted into the beginnings of a smile, though it never quite eventuated. In fact he looked downright serious. Heart beating so loud she was certain he could hear it too, Paige took a breath to say goodnight, but Gabe cut her off, eating up the space between them with three long strides. Barefoot, she had to look up so far to meet his eyes.

'When will I see you again?' he asked.

Paige's breath hitched in her throat. Apart from the party invite, it was the first time either of them had even come close to suggesting making actual plans. 'Soon enough, if the past few days are anything to go by,' she said, trying for sassy, but when her voice came out all husky she failed miserably.

'Good point. But I was thinking more along the lines of dinner.'

'Dinner?' Paige asked, her voice rising in her complete surprise. 'Like a proper date?'

Gabe nodded, serious face well and truly in place.

A date? A *date*. A date. Experience said no way. Gabe was a nomad. She'd recognised the impatience in his eye the moment she'd first seen him. If she hadn't learned to keep a man like that at arm's length from watching her mum watch her dad walk away, time and time again, then she was an out and out fool.

Of course, there was the small fact that Nate was in the process of trying to get Gabe to stay...

'Paige,' Gabe said, the tone of his voice making it clear he wanted an answer.

While her subconscious argued back and forth, all she could do was go with her gut. And it turned out that her gut, like the rest of her body, wanted Gabe.

'Okay. Let's do it.'

'Good,' he said on a hard shot of outward breath. 'I'll call to set it up.'

Gabe slid a finger beneath her chin, and kissed her gently. Tenderly. Then his tongue swept into her mouth and she curled her fingers into his sweater and held on for dear life.

Then with a shake of his head, and a growl that told her it took everything he had to leave it at that, he turned and disappeared into the stairwell, a flash of dark clothing, and huge shoulders, and powerful strides. Leaving Paige blinking into the bright empty hallway.

At the start of the night her biggest hope had been that their sizzle didn't fizzle in public. Now he'd asked her on a date. She'd wished for a guy to end her dating drought. She had nobody to blame but herself.

SEVEN

——

Paige had just sat down to cocktails with Mae and Clint at the sparkly pink Oo La La bar on Church Street when she got the call she'd been telling herself she hadn't been waiting for all day.

She held up a finger to excuse herself, slipped off the stool, and headed out into the icy Melbourne night. She stuck her spare hand under her armpit and banged her feet against the ground in an effort to keep warm as she answered her mobile.

'Hey, Gabe!' Paige scrunched up her face. Even in the age of number display, she should have at least feigned nonchalance.

As Gabe's rich laughter rumbled down the phone she realised she needn't have worried about the cold; every time she heard that voice a wave of heat followed in its wake.

'What's up?' she asked. As if she didn't know that either! She bit her lip to stop herself from saying anything else daft.

'I do believe I promised you dinner,' he said.

'Right. So you did.' There, that was better. Now she might get away with him not guessing she'd spent much of her Saturday daydreaming about where he might take her. Or what she might wear. If Gabe's sweet tooth was enough to make them last till dessert. Or if his taste for her was stronger still.

A tram thundered noisily down the street, sparks flinting off the overhead cables and disappearing into the inky blackness above. Paige pressed the phone to her right ear, and a finger in the left. 'I'm sorry, I missed that last part.'

'I said we'll have to have a rain check.'

Her feet stopped stamping and she came over all still.

'I'm in Sydney for work. Flew down first thing this morning. Not sure when I'll be back.'

He was in Sydney? A thousand miles away and he hadn't even told her he was going? He hadn't even had anything like this on the cards as far as she knew. Because she didn't known much of anything? Unless he'd simply changed his mind. Maybe his claustrophobia was so bad he'd only asked in the aftermath of post survival euphoria!

'Paige? Can you hear me?'

'Yeah. I got that,' she said. She rubbed at a spot under her ribs where she suddenly felt as if someone were poking her with a chopstick. 'Cool. I understand. I've got so much going on at work this week as it is. I guess I'll catch you when you get—'

'Paige.' He cut her off, his deep drawl pouring through her like melted chocolate.

'Yep?' She closed her eyes and slapped herself several times on the forehead for good measure. When she opened her eyes it was to see a couple, arms linked, scooting as far around her on the footpath as possible. She sent them a sorry smile but they were jogging too fast to see.

'I'll be back in a couple of days, and then I'm sure we can squeeze in a night out if we both try real hard.'

He didn't say, *'before I leave for good,'* but it was out there, like a big black piano waiting to fall down on her head. Paige pressed the heel of her palm to her chest as the chopstick beneath her ribs grew thorns.

'I'll call when I know more,' Gabe said.

'Sure. Fine. Or not. Whatever. Honestly, I'm cool either way.'

Gabe laughed again, the smooth deep sound vibrating down her arm and landing with a warm thud deep in her belly. 'I'll call,' he promised, 'even if you're cool either way.'

'Okay,' she said on a long drawn out breath.

'Goodnight, Paige.' He rang off.

Paige turned towards the bar, but there her boots stopped short. She tapped her phone against her front teeth, her eyes misting over to the soft pink light spilling through the windows of the funky cocktail bar as she forced herself to think.

Good God, had she really floated the idea that Gabe was in Sydney avoiding her? She needed to get a grip. A man she wasn't attached to had merely postponed a date that till the night before had never even been on the cards. And yet her heart thumped at triple its normal pace. That wasn't her. She did not obsess about men she couldn't have. She was *not* her mother...

No. Time apart was the exact wake-up call she needed. Her life had been plenty satisfying before Gabe Hamilton moseyed into her lift and into her life, and she could do with a few days without him to remind her of that.

She breathed deep, the thin cold air slipping into her bloodstream, and she felt far less wobbly than she had a minute earlier. In fact she felt positively urbane. Then the extreme mixed scents of Richmond's Asiatic restaurant row hit the back of her throat and hunger followed in its wake. Teeth chattering, she hustled back inside the bar.

'Trouble in paradise?' Mae asked as Paige plonked herself back on her stool.

Paige opened her mouth to say everything was fine, but Mae's open palm stopped her in her tracks.

Mae said, 'Let me tell you a little story while you consider your answer. There I was the other night, enjoying my mini-quiche at your gorgeous neighbour's housewarming, when I spotted you and the hot pirate, looking all cosy. I barely had time to jab Clint in the ribs when you were off, running for the door as if you couldn't wait to find somewhere private in which to tear one another's clothes off.'

Paige blinked down into her milky cocktail as the heat rose in her cheeks; a healthy mix of mortification that if Mae had noticed there was a good chance others had too, and regret that Mae knew she'd been keeping her fling with Gabe a secret.

'So what's going on with the two of you?' Mae asked.

'Nothing,' Paige insisted. 'Okay, something. But not what you think.'

'Why didn't you tell me?'

'It all happened so fast.'

'So fast you couldn't send me a text? Preferably with image attached.'

Paige frowned at Mae's pink cocktail, and tried to find an answer her best friend might understand, and couldn't. 'Honestly, I don't know why I didn't tell you. Maybe because I wasn't quite sure what to say. I'm still not.'

'Sounds serious.'

'Lord, no! It's a fling. That much I am sure of.'

'You've had flings before, Miss Paige. Before Clint came along the two of us were the queens of the no-strings fling and you never kept it from me before. So what made this one different?'

She risked looking at Mae, and saw the one person in the world who knew her best. Her next breath out felt awash with relief that the truth was out, tempered by a little stab of heartache that she'd found it so hard to tell her.

She leaned forward, and wrapped her fingers around her cold glass. 'Maybe it's that from the moment I met him it *felt* different. Which has been thrilling, but also kind of terrifying. I might be struggling a bit with remembering where my limits lie.'

'Maybe you're struggling because, with him, you don't want limits.'

Paige let herself wonder for about half a second before she remembered the unbearable feeling of the chopstick jabbing her under the ribs. She shook her head. 'Oh, no. With this one I want them more than ever.'

Mae nibbled at the inside of her cheek a few moments as if she was grappling with some inner turmoil, before leaning over and wrapping cool hands around Paige's. 'I know you like putting your life into neat separate little boxes, Paige—work, home, friends, lovers—and I get why. Having them in boxes makes them feel like they're under your control. I used to be the same way. And then I met Clint.'

Paige got her usual tummy ache at the mere mention of Clint's name, only this time the jab of the chopstick under the ribs joined it. Which made no sense at all.

Oblivious, Mae went on. 'I thought he was goofy and shy and way too sweet for the likes of me. I could have put him in that easy-to-ignore box on day dot and that would have been that. But I took a chance instead. I let him see me, and let myself see him. And look at us now.'

Paige wriggled on her stool, not liking talking about Clint any more than she had about Gabe. Because she hoped so hard that Mae could rise above the statistics, and genetics, and history and be happy for ever after? All of a sudden that theory didn't hold water.

She gave herself a mental shake. One thing at a time. This current dilemma was about her. And Gabe. Even the mere thought of him had her breathing out long and slow.

Paige waved her hands in front of her face. 'I know in your loved-up state you're seeing cupid's arrows flying all over the place, but it's not like that. I assure you. It's sex. Pure and simple. Well, to be honest it's not so pure or so simple.'

Finally Mae stopped looking at her as if she was try-ing to see right into her soul. Her voice a low growl, Mae said, 'Now, you're talkin'. Details. You owe me.'

Paige figured she did, and then some. And gossip-ing like this felt so good, like the old days. 'So what do you want to know?'

'Do you have actual conversations in between bouts of athletic lust?'

'Sometimes. Sometimes we don't want to waste our breath.'

'Phew.' Mae rested her elbow on the table and her chin on her upturned palm. 'Do you catch yourself daydreaming about him? About his belly button, the whirl of hair behind his right ear, the way his eyes go all dark and dreamy when he sees you?'

Paige raised an eyebrow. 'Clearly *you* do.'

'Ha! So are you seeing anyone else?'

'No,' Paige answered before she'd even noticed Mae's change of tack, or the knowing gleam in her eye. Dam-mit.

'Do you want to?' Mae asked.

Paige sat up straighter. 'Where's Clint?'

'At the bar.'

'Good, I need another drink.'

'I'll bet you do.' Mae gave Paige's foot a quick nudge under the table. 'I know you, Paige. You are doing your absolute all to avoid even considering it, but I'm liv-ing proof that happily ever afters can happen, even to those who don't believe in them. And that's the last I'll say about that.'

Mae mimed zipping her mouth shut tight as Clint

returned with a beer for himself, another pink drink for Mae, and a Midori Splice for Paige.

'You looked like you might need it,' he said, before he slumped back onto his stool and closed his eyes as if he was seriously about to have a nap right there in the middle of the bar.

Paige should have thanked her lucky stars that Clint's arrival had saved her from answering any more of Mae's questions. But watching Mae's eyes constantly swerving back to her fiancé, her finger running distractedly across the rim of her cocktail glass, her cheeks warm and pink, a small smile curving at her mouth, Paige felt as if she was witnessing something so intimate she ought to look away.

But she found she couldn't.

Did Mae really believe they could love each other through everything? Through fights and ambivalence? Through having kids and demanding jobs? Through the times they were in each other's pockets every minute of the day and the times they spent apart? Through the times they'd inevitably hurt one another in moments of boredom, exhaustion, self-absorption?

Her parents hadn't. Not even close. For them it had simply been too hard. So Paige just couldn't make herself believe. Even when Clint opened one eye and gave Mae a warm lazy smile, and it was like being *this* close to the real thing Paige could almost touch it.

She took a hard gulp of her cocktail, barely tasting it as her mind shifted to the one secret she hadn't dared share with Mae, the secret she'd refused to even admit to herself until that quiet moment in the noisy bar.

She felt things for Gabe. Soft, gentle, warm things.

She didn't believe it would last. She didn't believe it was about anything other than chemistry. But it terrified her to the soles of her boots.

In the end Gabe was gone a little over a week.

Paige was thrilled at how much she got done with all that extra time! She'd done her tax. She'd rearranged her lounge-room, twice. Made her way through every level of Angry Birds. Caught up with Mae, and Clint, another two times. And she'd thrown herself into work with a gusto she hadn't felt for months, shining up her proposal to shoot the summer catalogue in Brazil until the thing about glowed.

Time apart had been a good thing for sure. She was in a good place. Sure again about what she was doing. And that she could handle it. Yet there was no denying the nerves that skittered through her belly the morning of the Monday he was due back.

She donned the new black lacy underwear she'd bought specially, then practically skipped into her walk-in robe to get dressed for the day and—

Instead of reaching for the work outfit she'd hung out the night before, her hand went to the white garment bag poking out from the deepest darkest corner of the cupboard and before she could stop herself she'd unzipped the bag containing her secret wedding dress with a rush.

The moment the weight of the daring concoction of chiffon, pearls, and lace filled her hands, something flipped a switch inside her and she had rough-housed the gown over her head. The satiny lining slid over her curves, cool and soft against her bare skin, then the hem dropped with a gentle swoosh to float over her bare toes. Her fingers shook as she guided the zip up her back until it stopped just below her shoulder blades.

Eyes closed, knees trembling, she turned to face the mirror behind her wardrobe door. She hoped desperately the thing swam on her, or the colour made her look jaundiced, or that she looked as if she belonged on the top of a toilet-paper roll like the doll her mum had in her downstairs bathroom.

'It's just a dress,' she whispered, her voice echoing in the cosy space. Yet when she opened her eyes it was to see herself through a sheen of tears.

Was this how Mae felt when she tried hers on? Beautiful, and special, and magical, and romantic, and hopeful? She didn't know, because she'd never asked. It was always Mae who brought up the wedding. Mae who came over to her place with bridal magazines. Mae who booked meetings with caterers and bands. Mae who had to work so hard to get Paige to even pretend to sound enthused.

Mae had motivation. Mae had found the thing they'd spent so many years convincing one another didn't exist. A man to trust. A man to hold. A man to love.

As if she were having an out-of-body experience, Paige watched her reflection with a feeling of detachment as a single tear slid down her cheek. And then everything came into such sharp focus she actually gasped.

Paige knew the moment it had happened. The moment her work had ceased to satisfy her. The moment she'd stopped dating. The moment her life had lurched out of her tightly held control.

It had happened with the first flash of Mae's pretty little solitaire as Mae had giddily told her Clint had proposed. The diamond dazzling her as the sun caught an edge, piercing her right through the middle, tearing every plan, every belief, every comfort she had that she wasn't alone in believing love wasn't priority number one.

She pressed the heels of her palms into her eyes, heat and tears squeezing past them.

What was *wrong* with her? Her best friend was in love. Getting married. Actually *happy*. Because of *that* her world had crumbled?

She'd always thought the hot spot that flared in her stomach whenever she looked at Mae and Clint together was fear for her friend. She'd been kidding herself. It was envy. Deep, torturous, craving certainty that she'd never experience even a tenth of the love and affection they shared. It had run so deep that for months she hadn't even been able to face going on a date that would only remind her she was destined to be alone.

The tears came so fast she began to sob. And then to choke. And then she couldn't breathe. Her lungs felt as if they were being squeezed from the inside out. The only way she'd ever breathe again was to get out of the damn dress.

She tugged at the straps, but they dug into her shoulders. She yanked at the deep neckline, but it wouldn't budge. Her trembling fingers wrenched at the zip at her back and—

She stilled, one foot braced indecorously on an ottoman, her arms doing some crazy pretzel move behind her.

The zip was stuck.

Like something out of a movie, the next hour of her life flashed before her eyes. She had to leave in ten minutes if she had a hope of getting to work on time. And first up that day? The final presentation of her Brazilian proposal.

Determination steeling her, Paige took a breath, sniffed back any remaining threads of self-pity, gripped the zip between unwavering fingers, and tugged.

Nada.

Argh! What was she going to do?

Mae and Clint lived only a couple of suburbs over, but in peak-hour traffic it would take for ever for one of them to get to her. The neighbour next door was in hospital getting a nose job. If she called on Mrs Addable upstairs her predicament would be all over the building before she even left the apartment.

Maybe she could wear the thing. She could cover most of it up. Her chartreuse beaded cardigan. Her cropped chocolate jacket. Her fringed grey cowboy boots. And accessories. Lots of fabulous accessories. She pictured the conference room: Callie holding court with the fawning assistants, Geoff hovering over the pastry tray trying desperately not to eat one, her assistant Susie looking up at her as if she were the bee's knees as she waltzed in...*wearing a wedding dress.*

With a sob Paige gave in and slumped to her back on her bed.

* * *

Gabe stood in the ground level foyer of the Botany Building, rubbing a hand across the back of his neck. It had been a hell of a week. The two other mobs who'd lined up to hear out the ramblings of a rabble of tech-nerds on nanotechnology applications had been the hardest competitors he'd been up against in an age. He'd been lit by the honest to goodness thrill of the chase, and the flicker of brilliance he'd spent his career chasing felt, if not imminent, then at least possible for the first time in a long time.

And yet Gabe felt unpredictably relieved at being back. The cold didn't seep into his bones like before. The trundle of trams didn't give him a twitch. And even the Gotham-esque skyline didn't appear quite so unforgivingly stark. In fact with the morning sun pouring over the jut of skyscrapers, glorious Finders Street train station, and the gleaming, snaking river, the city had looked downright pretty.

Maybe he'd missed his bed, with its him-shaped dent. Or maybe he'd missed what could have been in his bed, all long and warm and languid, a warm smile lighting up her deep blue eyes, her lush pink mouth—

The lift binged.

Gabe discreetly repositioned himself. Whoever might be in the lift didn't need to see how a week without Paige in his bed had affected him. But without even opening its doors, the lift headed back up without him.

A muscle twitched in his cheek. 'Now, this I didn't miss.'

The lift paused on the eighth floor. Paige's floor. He checked his watch. She might not yet have left for work. He could drop in. Say 'hi'. Shore up their plans for dinner that night. He actually laughed out loud. As if he'd be able to stop at just that.

No, he needed to get into the office to debrief Nate on the deal. He needed to get back to the piles of paperwork that needing reading before he signed on the dotted line to list BonaVenture on the stock market. So that he could get out there again, back amongst the sharks where he belonged.

And yet as he eyeballed the lift his mind didn't wander to the big wide world waiting for him. His fingers twitched at the thought of burying themselves in masses of silken blonde hair. His mouth watered as he imagined the sweet taste of soft pink lips. He hardened at the thought of burying himself deep inside a woman who knew how to take him to the brink and right on over the other side.

He checked his watch again. His feet twitched and he stared at the lift, as if eyeballing it would make it come back to him.

Screw it.

Three long strides took him to the door to the stairs; he pushed through and took them two at a time, a surge of adrenalin all but giving him wings. His blood pumping hard through his veins as he got ever closer to number eight.

He reached her floor, jogged to her apartment, and, before he could talk himself out of it, banged on her door with a closed fist, feeling a connection to his caveman ancestors. If he was able to do more than grunt before kissing that heavenly mouth of hers he'd deserve a damn medal.

She was home. The shuffle of bare feet on her polished wood floor brought on a heavy heat in his groin. 'Paige,' he called, his voice as gruff as a bear's. 'It's me.'

Then, listen as he might, he heard nothing, not even a breath. He hadn't imagined it, had he? Conjuring up sounds of her that weren't even there? He started as the doorknob squeaked and turned in its socket. Then the door opened as if in slow motion.

It had been barely a week since he'd seen her, yet the moment he looked into her beautiful face his heart skipped a beat. He'd heard the expression, but before that moment he'd not known it felt like stepping off the top of a tall building with only a faint hope there'd be a dozen firemen waiting below with a big trampoline.

Paige blinked at him, her gorgeous blue eyes smoky with smudged eyeliner. Her hair was all a tumble. Her skin flushed pink. The woman looked so gorgeously rumpled he throbbed for her, and it took every effort not to throw her over his shoulder and toss her down on the bed and take her before they'd even said hello.

Cleary a glutton for punishment, he slid his gaze down her gorgeous body to find it encased in—

What the—?

He blinked. And again.

Well, he thought as his libido limped into hiding as though it had been kicked where it hurt most, *you don't see that every day.*

EIGHT

___

'**Are we a** tad overdressed for this time of the morning?' Gabe asked.

'What do you think?' Paige asked, before swallowing so hard the tendons on her neck looked about to snap.

'I think you're wearing a wedding dress.' Even as he said the words a pulse began to beat in his temple. 'Is it yours?'

After a long second she nodded, her eyes like those of a puppy who'd been kicked. As if *she* were the one who should be feeling hard done by, not the guy she was sleeping with who'd just come back from a week away to find himself staring down a bride.

Right. Okay. Think. Not an easy thing to do considering he was fighting against the unwieldy mix of raging lust and abject horror wrestling inside him.

'And you're wearing it because...' *You've been married before? You're getting married today? You missed me that much...?*

Wow. Had everything somehow been leading to

this? No matter all the safeguards he'd put in place, had he been outfoxed again? Should he have paid more heed to Hitchcock's warnings after all? He'd give her a minute to explain. Two at most. And if he wasn't a hundred and ten per cent thrilled with the answers he was outta there.

'The zip's stuck!' She turned, lifted her hair and flashed him an expanse of beautiful back. And creamy-coloured lace, and pearl looking things and—

Gabe lifted his eyes to the ceiling. 'That's not exactly... I meant why do you own a...you know?'

'Took you long enough to ask.'

Gabe was fairly sure he'd only been at her apartment door for a minute but apparently he'd passed through the looking glass, so who knew? 'Forgive me if my mind's working at about thirty per cent velocity, but what the hell are you talking about?'

'Oh, come on. You knew about the dress.'

Gabe shook his head, hard, hoping it might send him back to the right dimension. 'What precisely am I meant to know about it?'

'That it exists. That it's mine. That I have a wedding dress in my possession.'

'Paige, I'm on the back foot here, with the dress, and the accusations, and the...dress. But I can honestly, hands down, say, I've never seen it before.'

'The day we met,' she shot back, eyes flashing, arms crossed beneath her breasts until they loomed above the deep V of the dress. 'I was carrying it in the lift.'

He opened his mouth to tell her she damn well wasn't, because there was no way in hell he'd have made a play for an *engaged* woman. Who needed that kind of drama? *Was* she engaged? No. He couldn't believe it. He shut his mouth, realising nothing good would come of any question he asked. And she didn't look in the mood for an argument. In fact she looked pretty close to a nervous breakdown.

Not exactly what he'd imagined their reunion might be like. Sure, he'd imagined heat, he'd imagined sweat, he'd not even dared hope to come close to losing consciousness. But right then, the only thing keeping him from bolting was the fact that the terror in Paige's eyes pretty much mirrored his own.

He tore off his beanie, unwound his scarf, rid himself of his jacket and threw them onto her kitchen diner. Then, hands shaking a little, he reached out, slowly, and curled his palms around her upper arms, careful not to touch the fabric wrapped lovingly around her body. Then he pressed himself inside her apartment and kicked the front door shut with his foot.

'Paige. Believe me when I tell you this. I don't recall you carrying anything that day.'

'You told Nate I tried to shut the door on your hand, but you don't remember me carrying a fluorescent white garment bag with 'Wedding Dress Fire Sale' in hot-pink neon writing slashed across the front of it?'

'I remember fine.' *The big blue bedroom eyes. The rumpled blonde hair. The legs that went all the way up. The sparks bouncing off the walls. The instant intense stab of desire that had made a mockery of his efforts to sleep his jet lag away.* 'I remember *you*.'

At that Paige blinked. Faster than a hummingbird's

wings. And then she breathed out, long and slow, as if she'd been holding her breath a real long time.

At the slow rise and fall of her chest his eyes defied him and slid down, noting how well the...thing fitted her, dipping at the front, hugging at the sides, sloping down her beautiful hips. If a man in a rented tux ever got to see *that* walking towards him down an aisle, he'd have no complaints.

But he would never be that man.

He liked Paige. She was funny, smart, great company, breath-taking in bed. But if this dress was some kind of sign, she was signalling the wrong man.

He wasn't a marrying man. Not even long-term-commitment guy. His priorities simply made it impossible. For as long as he could remember his ambitions had been clear-cut: to work hard and make his gran proud. After his one monumental hiccup, he'd poured all of himself into fixing that mistake. Never making the same one again.

And he wasn't here. Was he? It didn't feel as though he was, but, considering his track record, who the hell knew?

He pinched the bridge of his nose, knowing there was no going forward—to the apartment, to work, or dinner, or even to her bed—till they cleared this all up.

Gabe slowly removed his hands and tucked them into the pockets of his old jeans and took a small step back. He lifted his eyes deliberately to hers. Her eyes were all liquid-blue, her lush mouth down-turned. She looked so forlorn, so...unbridely, it was almost laughable. Almost.

He motioned with his chin to the small kitchen

table. 'Sit.' She sat. Gabe sat too, though far enough away so as not to touch. 'So do you want to tell me what this is all about so I can stop looking over my shoulder for the priest?'

'Really?'

'More than you know.'

'Okay,' she said, then after a big deep shaky breath went on. 'So I'd been shopping with Mae to find her wedding dress the morning before we met, and I saw this dress and felt like I'd never breathe again if I didn't take it home. Not out of some deep and abiding desire to get married. I've never been one of those girls who always wanted to get married. On the contrary. So we can clear that up.'

'Okay,' he said, feeling far from clear.

Then Paige looked down, a swing of fair hair falling over her face, all her usual va va voom seeping out of her as she stared at some unknown spot on the table. 'Turns out Mae getting married has really thrown me. More than I'd realised until about half an hour ago. I've been completely out of sync since she got engaged. We've been in one another's pockets for such a long time. And now she's...not mine any more.' She held out her hands as if she'd lost something then settled back into her slump. 'I've been going through the motions ever since. With Mae. At work. Not dating.' Her eyes slid to his, her long dark lashes all crazy and clumped together. 'You're the first guy I've seen since it happened.'

The emphasis on the word 'seen' brought a flare of heat to his groin. When he shifted on the chair Paige noticed, and her mouth flickered into the first smile of the day.

'Mae had a theory about why I bought the dress,' she went on, 'and it was easier to believe that than to believe the truth. That I was jealous of her. Not the marriage bit, the happiness bit. So I kind of wished for you. And then a minute later you stuck your fingers through the lift door.'

'I'm sorry... You wished for me?'

Sass put some sinew into her slump as she flicked her fringe off her face, and lifted one saucy shoulder. The flare of heat spread till it roared through his blood with the speed and intent of a bush fire.

'Well, not *you* in particular,' she said. 'A man who... Well, a man. Mae's theory for why I bought the dress was that I needed to get some.'

Gabe's mouth turned dry at the thought...for about half a second. Then saliva pooled beneath his tongue and he had to physically press himself back into the chair so as not to go right ahead and give her what Mae thought she needed.

Paige slowly eased herself upright, leaned back in her chair, and looked him dead in the eye, and he realised she hadn't been kidding. If any other man had walked into the lift at that precise moment she would have been sitting at her kitchen table sending some other guy hard with desire with those burning baby blues of hers.

No way. It wouldn't have been the same. The way they fitted was chemical. One in a million. Thus worth pursuing to the edges of his limits. Clearly, or

he wouldn't still be sitting there while she wore a wedding dress.

He leaned forward, keeping her gaze connected to
his. 'And now that you have...got some, how are you
doing?'

Paige tilted an eyebrow, before wafting a hand past
her lace-covered curves. 'How do you think I'm doing?'

'Fair enough.' Gabe rubbed his fingers into his eyes
to clear the image that was making it hard for him to
see straight. 'And do you try it on every morning—?'

'Good God, no! This was the first time *ever*. Don't
think I ever had any intention of you finding me like
this. This is my worst nightmare. And I can't fathom
why *you're* still sitting here and not halfway to anywhere else but here!'

She had him there. He'd help her get the dress off
then vamoose. Go home. Go to work. Put some space
between them so that he could think.

He shoved back the chair so hard it squeaked on
the pale floorboards. He motioned to her with a flick
of his fingers. 'Come on.'

'What?'

'You said that thing was stuck.'

She nodded. 'The zip. It's caught on something. I
tried tugging, and shimmying it over my head, but it
fits like a glove.'

It did that. 'Then let's get you free of it, shall we?'

Paige stood, and turned her back to him.

Swallowing down the bile rising in his throat at
the connotations of ridding a beautiful woman of a
wedding dress, Gabe forced his eyes to move to the

dress to find a paper clip had been bent through the eye of the zip.

His tension melted a little. At least now he could be certain she'd had a go at taking the thing off. As for the rest? Everyone had weaknesses, and if hers was for a combination of lace and pearly-looking things, then it beat smoking. Just.

'Do you need me to move at all?' she asked, lifting her hair away from her neck, the scent of her shampoo wafting past his nose for the first time in days. The interplay of muscle across her back made his fingers feel fat and useless as blood left his extremities to pour into his groin.

He reached for the zip, the backs of his fingers brushing across her warm skin. Her muscles twitched at even his slightest touch. A few strands of hair fell to slide against the back of his hand and, God help him, delicate shocks prickled down his arms landing with a rock-hard thud in his pants.

'You want this thing off or not?' he asked, his voice gruff.

'I do.'

'Then stop wriggling.'

She stilled. And there were a few long moments in which the only sound was the shuffle of satin on her skin as the hopeless zipper refused to budge.

'I had an outfit,' she said. 'For tonight.'

'Another one?'

Her laughter was husky, telling him he wasn't the only one affected by the fact that he was, to all intents and purposes, trying to get her naked. The sound vibrated through him, morphing into a *whump whump whump* that pulsed through his veins.

'Quite something, this outfit of mine. Red, sleek, no zip in sight.'

He swallowed down the lust rising from the bottoms of his feet all the way to the back of his throat. The phenomenal pull of desire he felt for her, despite the wedding attire, gave him one last pause.

Did he want her too much? To the detriment of his own sense? His own self-interest? He listened to his gut, and listened hard. But even his deeply scarred conscience couldn't go there. She was habit-forming, but the hold she had over him was unintentional. And all the more dangerous because of it? Not so long as they both knew the score. He'd just have to make sure she never forgot it. Him either.

'Careful,' she cried out suddenly when the sound of over-stretched fabric rent the silence. Then like the collapse of a dam, the zip gave way. The dress tipped over her shoulders and she scooped it to her chest, but not before he'd caught a glimpse of a strapless black lace bra and a hint of matching G-string.

'Oh, come on!' she said, turning and staring down at the dress so that her breasts pressed together. 'I'd been working on that damn thing for half an hour! It clearly hates me. Well, I hate it right on back. It's so going straight to Good Will after this.'

'Nah,' he said, his voice rough as sand, 'I have the touch.'

She glanced up at him, her chest pinking as she realised the direction of his gaze. And he was more than half hard. When their eyes met, her bottom lip was tucked between her teeth, and her naked toes curled over one another under the pool of material at her feet.

And Gabe knew he wasn't going anywhere.

A half-second after he moved for her, she let the dress go and was in his arms. Clinging to him as he devoured her with his mouth. Tasting her neck, his tongue tracing the line of her jaw, teeth nipping at her ear. When he slid his hands to cup her backside it was to find the dress was thankfully gone, leaving him with her hot bare skin and a strip of lace.

When he lay her back on the table, atop his jacket and scarf, she was pink all over. A pulse beating fast in her neck. Her lips moist from his kiss. Her eyes so hot he could barely make out a thin circle of blue. She grabbed him by the beltline, tugging him between her legs, wrapping her thighs about him as she whipped his button fly open with one rough yank.

With a growl he buried his face in her breasts. Drinking in the scent of her till his lungs were full. When he palmed her breast she arched off the table.

Lust filled him so thick and rich his vision was a pinprick. His focus concentrated on a bead of perspiration running down her torso. The jump of her muscles as his hands encircled her waist. Her gasp as he pressed a kiss to her navel. The grip of her hands in his hair as he sank his teeth into her hipbone. The way she trembled as he ran a thumb along the strip of soft black lace.

Holding onto the thinnest thread of control, he pressed her thighs apart and kissed her. She flung an arm over her eyes and let her thighs fall apart all the way. He tugged the slip of lace aside and took her in his mouth, tasting, bringing her to the edge before pressing soft kisses to her inner thigh. When she begged him to never stop, he never did, and when she came it was with such abandon he almost came right along with her.

Fumbling for his wallet, he took for ever before he found a condom. Sheathed, he hovered over her, waiting until her eyes found his, glints of fire, before he sank into her. Pressing into her velvet heat, deeper and deeper. The walls of her body gripping him like nothing else he'd ever known. One hand around the top of the round table, the other on his hip, she sucked in short sharp breaths. When pleasure gripped him from the inside out his eyes squeezed shut and he heard himself yell her name as he came.

As the world slowly came back into focus Gabe's head cleared. And it was as if the hard and fast sex had knocked something loose.

He looked into her eyes, to find them dark, liquid, sated, making him hard for her all over again. Knowing it, she grinned, and stretched her arms over her head, letting them dangle over the edge of the table.

Willing himself to keep it together another moment, he asked about the one part of the morning that hadn't made some sort of crazy sense. 'All this time you thought I thought you owned a wedding dress, and you therefore believed that *I* believed you were possibly about to be married.'

She looked up at him from under her lashes. 'Possibly.'

He braced an arm against the kitchen table. 'And that was *okay* with you?'

'Not normally. But remember I was a girl with not a lot of experience in happily ever afters who'd just bought a wedding dress. I needed to do something equally desperate to counteract the first act.'

Gabe blinked at her. A glint had made it through the sexual haze in her blue bedroom eyes. She was making jokes? 'Hell, Paige. Consider what you've put me through so far this morning and give me the slightest break, okay?'

She lifted a knee to brace herself, her inner thigh accidentally sliding along the outside of his leg. Or maybe not so accidentally. He was fast learning the woman had hidden facets.

'Gabe, I've dated guys who aren't jerks and they've still jerked me around. So I figured dipping my toes back into the dating pool with a jerk there'd be no nasty surprises.'

'Did you call me a jerk?' Gabe pushed himself to standing, found his jeans and yanked them up, buttoned them, and ran a hand up the back of his neck. His head was starting to thud.

'No. No!' she said, bracing herself on her elbows, the long, lean, rumpled, semi-naked length of her draped over the table. 'Honestly, there's nothing about you that screams jerk. Or whispers it even. But, come on. You were all big and dark and stubbled and dishevelled from your flight. Could you blame me for not jumping straight to "Mr Nice Guy"?'

His default position, to get annoyed and stay that way, flickered to life. But the thing was she was right. She'd seen him at his irritable worst and thought him unapproachable. He had seen a leggy blonde and thought SEX! They'd both been spot on.

But, just in case, he looked back at her, right into her eyes, looking for something else. The opposite of what he'd always been most afraid of. A sign of hope. Of expectation. A sign that she was deeper into this thing than he was.

'Yikes! Is that the time?' she said before he had the chance and Paige wriggled off the table and made a mad dash for what must have been her bedroom. The shower turned on. Two minutes later she was out. Dressed in tight black pants, black T-shirt, black man-eater boots, a swirly grey jacket that made her eyes look like the clearest summer sky.

With a hairpin between her teeth as she tamed her long hair up into a quick neat bun, she said, 'I have to run. So so late. Big big meeting. Last chance to convince Callie to let me shoot the summer catalogue in Brazil.'

He grabbed her hand as she fled past. She spun to look at him, her brows raised in question. How to put this delicately? 'I was never one of those boys who played "getting married" dress-ups when I was a kid either. Just so you know.'

She cocked her head, a grin sliding onto her mouth. 'Good to know. And considering your namesake, and your extensive knowledge of Doris Day movies, I'd have thought a penchant for playing bride and groom might have been one step too far.'

Damn, he thought. Some girl he'd found himself. Or had she conjured him after all? Either way... *Damn.*

'See you tonight?' she asked.

He nodded.

She planted a kiss on his lips. *Domestic,* he thought, not sure how it made him feel, before she pressed up on her heels, slid a hand into the back of his hair and the kiss deepened until blood was roaring through his head once again.

Who knew how long it was before she unpeeled herself from his front, blew a stray strand of hair from her forehead, and grinned?

'Welcome home. Lock up on your way out.' And she was gone.

When the sound of the slamming front door stopped echoing through the apartment, Gabe looked around, realising belatedly it was the first time he'd been inside. Pale furnishings. Lots of books, mostly coffee table and recipe. No prints on the walls, only photos; blown up, framed well. Photos of her travels, laughing raucously with Mae, with a cool-looking blonde who must have been her mother.

The rest wasn't overly garnished as he had imagined it might be, considering her job and her admitted penchant for scatter cushions. It was soft, elegant, warm. A haven not a showroom. It was her. Which gave him the impression that inviting someone into her home was akin to inviting someone into her life.

A strange feeling came over him then. Tightness. Darkness. Anticlimax.

She'd never invited him in. Not once. He'd had to practically bang her door down like some testosterone-laden caveman to get inside.

He'd thought himself in charge of the tempo of this thing. But from day one she'd come to him, and left him, on her terms. He'd let her because it was easy. He'd let her because it was hot.

He grabbed his stuff before letting himself out, locking the door behind him. As the lift took its sweet time in collecting him he stared unseeingly at his scowling face in the silver doors of the lift.

He told himself that after the rest of the morning's debacles it shouldn't have even registered on his list of things to give a flying hoot about. That since they were having a casual fling it shouldn't damn well matter at all where they were doing the flinging and where they weren't. But if the ball of lead that had taken up residence in his gut was anything to go by, apparently it damn well did.

NINE

Gabe sat at his big gleaming desk in his vast and spartan office at BonaVenture later that day, ignoring yet more paperwork. His desk was annoying him too much to concentrate. The colour of the walls was making him twitch. Not that he wanted to shop online for interior decorations ever again. When he'd done so for the party he'd actually felt his balls shrink a size.

Instead he sat there and fumed and wondered, if Paige's apartment was such a clear reflection of her, then what did this office and his apartment say about him that his oldest friend thought he'd find them comfortable?

He sank his face into his hands and rubbed his temples with his thumbs. Since when had he ever wanted to be *comfortable*? For as long as he could remember, he'd sought brilliance in his life. He'd wanted to make an impression. Every way, every day. Nothing like having your parents die young to show a kid that every moment counted.

And somehow that had twisted into a footloose existence where the only thing that had his lasting imprint on it was a bed.

It was a hard truth to admit. Harder still to know what, if anything, he planned to do about it. Because no matter how far his life was from his original plans, it worked. Look at the success that had come of it. Did he even have the right to want to change things now?

When Nate came into his office followed by his assistant and a tray of coffee and doughnuts, like any cornered animal, Gabe lashed out. 'Tell me we're nearly done,' he growled.

'But that would be a lie,' Nate said. The assistant smartly left.

'I've read everything you've put in front of me. Listened to a dozen different experts. I'm not sure what else can be brought to the table. Hell, I'll take a meeting with a bearded lady and her psychic monkey if that'll convince you I'm up to speed.'

The sober leather chair on the other side of Gabe's desk squeaked as Nate lowered himself into it. 'I hoped your time away would eventually wear down the chip on your shoulder. Seems it's burnished it to a shine.'

Gabe glanced across at Nate, a fighting muscle jumping under his left eye, to find Nate looking tired. More than tired, he looked older. As if the years, the business, had taken their toll on him too. Gabe wrestled his inner bear back into his cave, because he knew he was partly to blame.

'I've been working on this move for nearly eight months,' Nate said, his eyes hidden as he rubbed his thumb and forefinger deep into his sockets. 'And all I've asked of you is a few days to play catch up.'

'I've hardly been twiddling my thumbs all this time.'

Nate stopped rubbing his eyes. Instead he looked at the ceiling, a muscle working in his jaw. 'Never said you had, mate. But I can't do this on my own. Well, I can, clearly.'

Gabe opened his mouth to refute that, but the steel in Nate's eyes stopped him.

'More to the point,' Nate said, 'I don't want to do it on my own. When we created this monster together everybody thought we were crazy. But we knew better. And it was fun. Even through the lean years. Look at what we achieved back then. Look at Alex. He wouldn't be the wunderkind he is now without us. And Harry's little website now practically runs the web. Then there were the McDumbass twins. What were we thinking there? Good times even when they were bad.'

Gabe's chest tightened. It had been so good. Exhilarating. Every decision fraught with risk and they'd only had their guts to guide them. And yet they'd got it so right time and time again. When had it all started to feel like so much work? He knew when. The one time he'd got it so very wrong.

Gabe leaned forward, placing his hands palm down on the table so as not to clench them into fists. 'We agreed back then that I'd take care of the research, you the schmoozing.'

'Mate,' Nate said, his smile wry. 'I let you sacrifice yourself for the sake of the company, because with your overblown sense of moral justice if I'd asked you to stay you'd have walked in a heartbeat thinking that's what was needed to save us all.'

'I—' Would have, for absolute sure. His gran's voice rang in his head: *Work hard, boy, and make me proud.* It was the compass by which he lived his life. And it felt as if he'd never stopped paying for the one time he'd lost his way.

In frustration, Gabe pushed at a pile of paperwork that shifted and swooshed to the floor. They both looked at it a moment, neither of them with the energy to clean it up.

'This is what it comes down to,' Nate said. 'List, or not. Sell, or don't. Make more money than we'll ever know what to do with overnight, or keep at it.'

'You got any dice on you?' Gabe said, and Nate's jaw clenched so hard pink spots broke out on his neck and cheeks.

'If that's how you want to choose, then that's your business. Just pick.' Nate thumped himself on the chest with a closed fist. 'It's not fun for me any more. How about you? When was the last time you found this fun?'

Gabe stared back.

'Yeah, that's pretty much what I thought.'

Gabe's insides felt so twisted he wasn't sure they'd ever find a way to untwist again. The desire to walk out of that door, only this time to never look back, burned within him. He knew he could go out on his own and survive fine. But something held him back. Whether it was his 'overblown moral compass' or something more elusive he could no longer be sure.

'Let's get out of here,' Nate said, standing and heading for the door. 'Get a drink. We can do this later. There's no rush.'

Gabe, who'd already decided a drink was a damn good idea, pushed himself to his feet. 'No rush? You spent the last ten minutes convincing me to make a decision!'

Nate's shoulders squared from behind as his fingers curled around the door. And with a rush Gabe understood.

Gabe said, 'Did you really think if you kept me here long enough I'd magically begin to realise all that I'd walked away from, and *stay*?'

Nate turned and leant against the doorjamb, a lazy smile spreading across his face, though there was no humour in it. 'Well, yeah, actually. It's time for you to come home. Because if you're not going to run this thing with me, then I'm out.'

Gabe blinked. He thought of what it had taken for him to come home. The red-eye flight. Sleeping on the floor of his apartment. The million memories, good bad and everything in between, clawing at him from every street corner. The bitter winter cold that never seemed to leave his bones unless he was with Paige—

His inner rant stopped there as if it had run head first into a brick wall.

Paige.

No matter the storm gathering around him, he couldn't add her to the fallout. The mere thought of her, warm and willing and wanton, was enough to quiet the worst of the noise building in his mind. His time with her was probably the reason he'd made it to this point without imploding. Or simply getting on a plane in the middle of the night. Or noticing Nate's now patently obvious motivation.

While she'd never even invited him in.

'So, old friend,' Nate said, cutting into his abstraction, 'do we take this thing out for a proper spin together? Or do we make more money than Midas and walk away?'

Nate gave the doorjamb a thump, and left, his voice sliding back through the door as if he were on the other side of the world as he said, 'Now hurry up. That drink won't wait all day.'

Paige gazed out of the window of the dark and sumptuous Rockpool Bar and Grill, the lights of the city glittering over her reflection in the glass. She couldn't remember ever feeling so relaxed on a first date. It was as if the breakthrough she'd had that morning about how she felt about Mae's engagement had unblocked all sorts of things inside her.

And then there was her date, who, for all intents and purposes, should have run screaming the minute she'd opened her door wearing a wedding dress that morning. But he'd stayed. Let her talk. Stripped her bare. Didn't flip out. That took some kind of man. Intrepid. Generous. Rock-solid. A Grown-Up. A man who knew himself so well he'd never have asked her on a date if there was anywhere else he'd rather be.

When he'd shown up at her apartment door earlier that evening in dark jeans, clean boots and tailored jacket over a grey shirt—his version of dressed up— she'd felt so *full* it had taken every ounce of energy to appear normal. But he didn't make her feel normal.

He made her feel safe. And for someone who spent her life waiting for the other shoe to drop, it was a trip.

She breathed deep, her nostrils filling with the mouth-watering scent of char-grilled beef, her gaze tripping over the mass of shiny black tables, past portraits of cattle hanging on the walls, to snatch glimpses of Gabe as he paced in the bar. After he pocketed his phone, and jogged up the steps to the dark restaurant, his eyes found hers. And her breath left her lungs in a whoosh as it always did when she found herself the subject of that stunning gaze.

'Sorry,' he grumbled as he sat across from her, 'work.'

She shrugged. Not much caring. She was glad to be there with a guy she liked and respected. One whose company, conversation, touch she'd missed acutely when he was away. But she'd survived just fine. She felt so urbane she could burst.

'You picked dessert?' he asked, flicking through the menu.

'You're not going to look at the appetisers first?'

'Never. Rule of thumb is only choose as much pre-dessert dinner as your chosen dessert will allow.'

'How you look like that when you eat how you do is beyond me.'

He glanced up at her, his eyes dark, but a smile tugging at the corner of his mouth. 'God loves me.'

'Clearly.' Her breath caught when he held her a gaze a fraction longer before his eyes swept slowly down her length before landing back on the dessert page. His smile turned to a grin as he said, 'There. Doughnuts. Lemon curd with vanilla apple and ice cream.'

When he flicked back to the steak selections, Paige leant her cheek in her palm and took her fill. The dark shirt straining across his huge shoulders. The golden lamps created gleaming streaks in his dark hair and shadows beneath his slashing cheekbones. Though she was sure the shadows beneath his eyes had nothing to do with the fall of the light.

He'd had a hard day, which she had no doubt had been made harder still by how it had begun. And yet here he was. A yearning kind of ache blossomed in her chest. And the same fullness she'd felt when he'd appeared at her door. Her heart beat a little faster to compensate.

Gabe looked up from his menu, and caught her staring. His eyebrows rose in question.

'So how is work?' she said, glancing away to find her wine. 'All big secret plans you're here to work on going well?'

A muscle jerked in his jaw and he frowned at the menu. 'Well enough.'

'Nearly done doing whatever it is you came here to do?' she asked.

He folded the menu and grabbed his drink, not even catching her eye as he said, 'Not soon enough.'

Whoa. She rubbed at the bare arm of her one-shouldered dress as she came out in a sudden case of goose bumps. 'So what *are* you working on, exactly?'

Gabe's eyes, darker still, slid back to hers. 'I can't discuss it.'

'Why the heck not?'

All he offered was a stubborn lift of his shoulder, and as the blissful warmth she'd been basking in all the long day took on a decided chill her contrary muscle kicked into full gear. She looked right back as she asked, 'What are you, some kind of spy?'

His mouth twitched, before flattening into a straight line. 'No. But my work can be...sensitive.'

She looked from one dark eye to the next, looking for a glimmer, a spark, something to tell her he was kidding and she'd missed the subtlety of his tone. But all she got was a big old wall. 'But you work in investments of some kind, right? Like a mini-bank.'

The pause before he nodded was so long Paige felt every beat of her heart, thumping short and tight. She waited, impatiently, until his distracted gaze caught on hers. 'I admit it's been a while since I've been on an actual date. But from memory it's the kind of event where people talk, with work being a common topic. So how about I go first? After the Brazil range we're going Parisienne for autumn. Your turn.'

She knew she was pushing him. His stillness couldn't have made it more obvious. But the leap it had taken for her to risk escalating what she felt for him by putting a name on it had been a leap of faith. In *this*. In him. She'd poured out her heart about the whole Mae thing. Something so deeply personal she hadn't even been able to admit it to herself. While he was acting like, well, pretty much the definition of a jerk.

She never should have agreed to do this. This wasn't what she'd signed up for, feeling all anxious and shaky and hopeful. She knew better than to make herself vulnerable to having her emotions screwed with by the actions of some guy.

She tucked her feet beneath her chair, ready to

throw down her napkin and get the hell out of there before she did something completely daft, like cry.

Until Gabe casually threw out, 'My work's not a game, Paige. Not all frou-frou and garnish. A lot of money's at stake. And reputations. Hundreds of people's futures.'

Paige's fingers still gripped the table, and, ignoring the *frou-frou and garnish* comment in an effort to stop herself from throwing her drink at him, she said, 'Good for you. But that doesn't explain the stoic silence on the subject.'

'The sharing of privileged information has serious consequences. I have to be extremely careful about who I talk to about my business particulars.'

It was so ridiculous she actually laughed out loud. And then a memory flickered into her head. 'Mae! Is this about that "insider trading" joke she made back at The Brasserie that night?'

Gabe didn't even blink as he said, 'She doesn't seem to be the most discreet person on the planet.'

Wow. Jerk didn't even *begin* to describe how he was acting. While she felt like the world's biggest fool.

'Enjoy your dessert,' Paige said, already on her feet as she grabbed her purse, threw twenty bucks for the drinks on the table. And then, in a last-ditch effort to appear sophisticated and not the trembly mess she felt, she added, 'Call me when you're done. I'll keep your side of my bed warm.'

She stalked out of the restaurant all but blind with rage and hurt and humiliation.

For a moment there, her heart pitter-pattering as she'd watched his beautiful head bent over the dessert menu, she'd actually let herself dream a little that maybe her soft, warm feelings for him meant something. That the fact that he'd seen her in a wedding dress and not fainted was a sign that something special was happening. Something precious. That her luck had changed.

Luck schmuck. For her to think differently about love, she'd need luck, a miracle, and the kind of change of heart for which she'd need a defibrillator, a thousand volts, and a near-death experience thrown in for good measure.

Gabe sat alone at the table long enough to finish his drink, even while it tasted bitter the whole way down. He had every intention of staying till the meal was done. There were doughnuts after all. Until out of the corner of his eye he saw the coat-check stubs, both of them, still on the table, meaning Paige was heading out there, into the freezing cold night, in an outfit that would give her frostbite.

'Dammit,' he growled, throwing a couple of hundred down to cover the table, before he grabbed the nearest waiter, jabbed the coat-check stubs in his hands and offered him another fifty if he got the coats in thirty seconds flat.

There was no denying he was angry that Paige had stormed off. Nothing he'd said had been untrue, even while he'd hardly gone out of his way to mollify her when it became clear she was getting upset. It was only because the urge to tell her everything she wanted to know had been so strong. After his run-in with Nate, the desire to get her take, to see the convoluted mess through her clear eyes, was too seductive.

And he'd been *there* before. Gripped by the need to open up to someone. He'd lost his gran just before he'd met Lydia, and had needed someone soft and warm to listen while he talked. And now he might be about to lose his company, his life's work, and again he found himself turning to a woman. A cool blonde, to make things that much more convoluted, especially when giving into that urge had screwed things up so roy-ally the first time.

Coats in hand, he shot out of the restaurant, down the long hallway, his long strides landing in the circles of golden light. He burst out into the Crown Casino complex, turned back the way they'd come.

Relief poured through him as he saw her on the next level down, halfway across the dark marble lobby and heading for the street. No way he could have missed her; not in that dress. Red, sleek, with a well-placed frill, a split up the side and one-bare shoulder, it had made it nearly impossible for him to keep his hands to himself, even while she pissed him off.

When she hit the busy night-time crowd outside he might never find her. He ran down the escalator, apolo-gising every two seconds, and he angled past the bus-tling crowd. And he caught up with her at the edge of the cab rank, standing tall, back straight as the valet hailed her a cab.

Gabe threw his coat over his elbow and placed hers over her shoulders. She didn't even flinch. As if she'd known he was there. As if her awareness of him was that attuned. Even as he tried to block out every feeling that realisation lit a spark of desire in his blood.

A cab swept up the crescent-shaped drive and Gabe whipped open the back door before it had even pulled to a halt. Paige slid inside and Gabe followed.

'Where to?' the cabbie asked.

When Gabe barked, 'Just drive,' the cabbie didn't argue. He set his meter to running and curved into traffic, whistling beneath his breath.

Paige slid her seat belt into place and looked out of the far window. Moonlight glinted off her hair. The city lights reflecting colour onto the curves of her red dress. It had slid halfway up her thighs, leaving her long legs smooth, tempting, crossed, knees pointed determinedly away from him.

'Paige, look at me.'

She shook her head, and if anything sat straighter. And like a slap to his subconscious he remembered the hurt twisting Paige's beautiful features as she'd thrown money on the table and offered him her bed for the night.

He fought the urge to kick the back of the cabbie's seat, and closed his eyes and prayed for patience. And help. Something he hadn't asked for in a long long time. He'd been so used to doing everything on his own. He'd had no choice. But if anyone out there was listening, he'd take whatever help he could get to make Paige listen.

The only thing close to help it got him was an insistent voice telling him to help himself. He ran a hand through his hair and said, 'I was an ass back there.'

Her shoulder lifted. But had her breath hitched in her throat?

He shifted to face her more fully. 'A stubborn, mulish ass. A jerk, if you will.'

Her shoulders slowly lowered. Silence hovered between them. And she turned, a half-turn, so he had her profile to contend with: long lashes, stunning eyes, red lips, skin like alabaster in the moonlight. She said, 'Too right.'

Okay, so she was talking to him. What more did he want? Hell, if he knew. But the idea of losing her right when things were so unstable at BonaVenture gave him such a tightness in his chest he gripped his fingers into a fist ready to give himself a good thump.

She breathed out long and slow, then in a voice with the kind of calm he'd have killed for in that moment she said, 'You have no idea the secrets I've kept in my life. I'm just saying.'

Gabe leant his arm along the back of the seat. 'Such as?'

She glanced at the cabbie, who was singing 'O Sole Mio' at the top of his lungs by then, before she realised the trap. Her blood-red lips curved into a smile, even while her forehead puckered into a frown. 'The big ones aren't secrets any more. Stuff about my mum and dad mostly. About his cheating. Mum knew it, I knew it, and we all pretended like it wasn't happening to keep the peace. Not so peaceful that, actually. Suffocating in fact. Much better now the secrets are out in the open. For all of us.'

Gabe watched her, eyes glinting, jaw tight, doing what she needed to do to rise above what amounted to a right royal mess of an example of what a relationship should be. His parents had died when he was young enough that he'd never had any kind of example of what a real loving relationship meant. His gran had tried to instil in him a sense of right and wrong, and had probably hoped that with that foundation he'd figure out the rest as he went along. Would she be disappointed how profoundly he had *not* figured it out? No doubt.

'It's fine,' Paige said into his silence. 'You don't have to tell me anything about your life if it makes you uncomfortable. Honestly.' But by the down-turned edges of her beautiful mouth he knew it was anything but fine.

Letting him in the cab had been her way of offering him a second chance. And he was going to take it. He needed a mental run-up. Even while the gist of his ignominy was public record, proof that even all these years later there was no getting away from it, talking about that time was…difficult. But if it came down to talking, or saying goodbye then and there…

Gabe wiped both damp hands down the sides of his thighs and talked. 'When I said the sharing of privileged information has serious consequences, it's because I know from direct experience. I talked too much once and it nearly cost me everything. So you can understand how I need to be careful about such things.'

'How did you screw up?'

Those big blue eyes of hers looked right into him. Drawing him in like a siren song. And even as he told himself the song was not meant for him he said, 'A woman. A blonde.'

Paige curled a swathe of her golden hair around a finger.

'No,' he said, answering her unspoken question. 'Not like you at all.'

Her eyes swept back to his, darker now. 'Girlfriend? Fiancée? Wife?'

'Friend. With benefits.'

A smile ghosted across her face. 'A bit like me, then.'

Gabe shook his head. 'Not unless you are my lead for a company I'm investing in, but spying for my direct competition at the same time. '

'Ouch.'

'Indeed. My rival, who couldn't find a good idea with two hands and a flashlight, leaked our relationship to the Australian Securities Commission, which led to an investigation.' Gabe looked out of the window. It had started to rain. The city lights now reflecting off the shining black road, the swish of tyres on the wet surface strangely soothing, considering how fast and frantic his heart was beating. 'We were cleared, but that kind of thing sticks.'

'Why did she do it?'

'Money, and a lot of it, for making me, a complete stranger to her before that point, look criminal at worst, incompetent at best. She wrote me a year or so after, explaining. Her husband had left her, and taken their kids and their cash and disappeared. She needed the money to find him.'

'She was desperate,' Paige said, as if it was no excuse, but maybe she understood a little.

Gabe turned back to find her knees had swung to face him and were mere millimetres from his own. His gaze fixated on the shadow beneath the stretch of red fabric at her thighs and his solar plexus clenched. 'You don't stumble into that kind of thing all the time in home wares?'

She moved a little, the dress rode higher and he had to grip the seat so as not to slide a hand up her warm thigh. She said, 'We did believe our catalogue images were stolen once. Turned out the intern had let a virus into the system when she was downloading a fake version of Angry Birds and it had eaten every image on file.'

'Not the same thing, then,' he said, his voice dry.

'Not so much.'

The cabbie finished his song, and in the silence Paige's chest rose and fell in a hypnotic rhythm. Now fixated on the silky frill that fluttered over her right breast every time she breathed, Gabe found himself saying, 'We were on top of the world right when it happened, and afterwards so near bankruptcy Nate was living on sandwiches and I was living on the crusts so that every spare cent could stay in the business. My only choice was to take myself out of the picture, while still doing the thing I did best, to give BonaVenture a chance. And I've been travelling ever since.'

Her long lashes swept swiftly against her soft cheeks and she looked long and hard at the middle of his chest. Every muscle within touching distance of that gaze clenched. 'How long ago was this?' she asked.

'Seven years.'

'About the time your gran Gabriella died.' Not a question. A statement. And, hell, if he couldn't remember even having told her.

His voice was gruff as he said, 'About then.'

'You were what? Mid-twenties? That's a lot to deal with. Especially for someone so young.'

Again with the understanding, he thought, but even he didn't fall for the nonchalant act. Instead he remembered with a piercing kind of immediacy how adrift he'd felt at that time. Anchorless. As if he'd lost his moral compass right as he'd hit the jackpot with money and success. Hell, no wonder he'd been easy pickings for the first woman who'd tried.

Her voice sang to him through the murky haze. 'BonaVenture Capital? Like the sponsors of the tennis? And that race before the Melbourne Cup, that's the BonaVenture Stakes, right?'

Gabe nodded again. Not that he'd known any of that before he'd read about it in the prospectus these last weeks.

'Well, it seems to me that, whatever you did, it worked. You lost your glass slipper for a while, but in the end you found it again.' And then she smiled, a soft, perceptive smile, and her eyes turned that particular shade of deep melting blue they only seemed to turn when they found him.

The image snapped something inside him. He felt it lodge in his ribs, like a Polaroid jammed in the corner of a mirror. A moment he should never forget. Then before he could stop himself he said, 'We're listing the company on the stock market. That's why I came back.'

He waited for the cold hard grip of panic to envelop him at what he'd revealed. But it never came. Instead he felt as if a fist that had been clenched deep inside him for as long as he could remember had unfurled and let go.

'Well, there you go. There's your happy ending,' she said, brightly, clearly having no idea what he'd given her. Or what he'd given himself. Then, 'I assume lips sealed on that one? No telling Mae?'

'Paige, about that—'

'Oh, shut up. She's the biggest blabber mouth this side of Antarctica. But I'm the only one who's allowed to say it. *Capiche?* And thanks for telling me.'

She leaned in then, as if it was the most natural thing in the world, and kissed him. Her lips were warm and sweet, the gentle flick of her tongue over his bottom lip incendiary.

When she pulled back she looked into his eyes and grinned. If her smudged lipstick was anything to go on he knew why. He was man enough to own a red pout for a kiss like that any day of the week. She unbuckled her belt, slid across the seat and leant on his shoulder. He belted her in, safe. Her scent curled into his nose, her sweet, luscious body nestled against his side, and he gave the cabbie directions to Docklands in a tone that meant the sooner the better.

He watched the familiar buildings slide by in silence. He'd always thought Melbourne looked its best in the rain. It brought lustre to the dark architecture. That night the city fair glittered back at him, like the facets of a jewel.

And Gabe realised whatever happened after this, without the secrets pressing against the inside of his skull as they had for so very long, for the first time in a long time he could see the flicker of brilliance at the corner of his eye.

Gabe walked Paige from the lift to her apartment door. He stood back, hands in his pockets, as she unlocked her front door, not wanting to fracture the delicate peace they somehow seemed to have carved out of the chaos of the evening.

Once the door was ajar she turned to him, her hand against his chest, small, warm, yet strong enough to make him feel as if it held his heart at bay. 'One more question.'

'Shoot.'

'This blonde who caused you all that trouble. Was she a natural blonde?'

He coughed out a laugh. 'Lydia?' he said, the name not creating the same swell of acid in his stomach as it used to. He thought about it. 'I'm not sure that she was.'

'Then there was your problem,' she said, her eyes meeting his. 'You should stick to natural blondes only in future.'

'I'll take that under advisement.'

They stood that way for a few beats, or a few minutes, how the hell was he to know? He was caught in those big blue eyes, and that gentle barely there touch had him rooted to the spot.

Then she stepped aside. 'Coming in?'

After the night they'd had Gabe wondered if it might be for the best to kiss her goodnight and head up to bed. To let the things they'd shared settle a while.

For about a tenth of a second he wondered, before

he stepped over her threshold and sank his hand into her glorious hair, and pressed his mouth, his body, his self as wholly against her as it was possible to do while upright and fully clothed.

He'd been invited after all.

TEN

——

Gabe burst into Nate's office the next morning at eight sharp. 'We're not selling!'

Nate looked up from his position on the floor by the window where he was twisting himself into some kind of pretzel shape on a mat.

Gabe's heels all but screeched on the rug as he pulled to a screaming halt. He cleared his throat and looked away. 'Sorry,' he said. 'I'll come back when you're not...doing that.'

Nate pulled himself neatly to standing and wiped a hand across his sweating brow. Motioning to the mat with an elbow as he downed half a bottle of water, he said, 'Yoga. Good for stress relief. You should try it.'

Gabe looked pointedly around Nate's princely office as he sank into a butter-soft leather couch. 'What have you got to be stressed about?'

Nate snorted. 'Now, what was it you stormed in here so early in the morning to declare?'

'Don't list the company,' Gabe said. 'Don't sell.'

Nate leant his backside against his desk and watched
Gabe for a long moment. Then he asked, 'Why?'

'I've been up all night rereading the contracts. All
of them.' Well, much of the night. The first half he'd
spent in Paige's bed. It was soft, cool, and he'd found
it nearly as difficult to leave it behind as his own. But
fuelled by a kind of boyish energy he hadn't felt in
years he'd felt a need to do the job he'd come there to
do. So he'd kissed her goodnight and gone back to his
apartment where he'd downed about a keg of coffee
and read. 'I needed to understand what we've achieved.
And what we'd be giving up. After what we've gone
through to get here? To hell with that.'

'Okay, then,' Nate said. He moved around his desk,
picked up the phone and asked his assistant to get
'John' on the phone as soon as he was in, then put
down the phone with a soft click. 'So you're in for the
long haul?'

'That's what it said on the beer coaster.'

At that Nate's cool finally gave way. He grinned
from ear to ear. And it was done. No over-thinking,
over-talking, making things more complicated than
they had to be. Just two men, making a decision that
set the course for the rest of their lives.

Nate moved to the far wall where a bar was hidden
discreetly inside a bookshelf. Like something Rock
Hudson would have had in his apartment in some old
Doris Day movie. Gran would have liked that. Would
have liked *this*. Gabe's mouth kicked into a half smile.

Gabe took the imported pony-necked beer on offer,
even while it was eight in the morning, and the two
men clinked bottles before taking a hearty swig. The

bubbles burned down Gabe's throat. Cold, sharp, invigorating. As if his body were fresh and hollow and waiting for the filling.

Nate said, 'Would have been more dramatic if you'd waited until the meeting with the Securities Commission.'

'Thought that's what I was doing, hence the volume of my proclamation.'

'They're due at nine. Did you actually read any of the internal memos I CC'd you these past weeks?'

'I figured if there was anything of grave importance you'd make sure I knew.'

Nate ran a hand over the back of his neck. 'Tell me again why I wanted you back?'

'My winning personality.'

Nate's eyebrows lifted till they all but disappeared into his hairline.

And so they continued, offending one another and knocking back beers until they were gloriously sloshed. When BonaVenture's lawyer called back a half-hour later, listening to the poor guy go off his nut was the most fun Gabe'd had at work in ages. And he wondered why it was he'd not come home sooner.

Paige pushed her way through the heavy glass doors leading to the head office of Ménage à Moi. She shielded her eyes against the overbright twinkles from the coloured glass chandelier above, her heels catching in the thick cream carpet as she trudged down the hall towards her office.

Her mind was like mud. Making love to Gabe half the night was only half the problem, as from the minute he'd left she'd had not a wink of sleep. After the drama of the date, the delicateness of the cab ride, and the sweet glorious way Gabe had made love to her all through the night, she'd been consumed by the sudden need to put it all into a neat little box. The feelings, and fears, and flutterings filling her as she'd lain there staring at her dark ceiling were so far beyond the bounds of her experience, if she didn't control them she feared they'd control her.

Crap, crap, crappity-crap!

Susie, her assistant, looked up from her cubicle with a start, and Paige realised she'd shouted that last bit out loud. She was re-e-eally going to have to stop doing that.

'Morning, boss. Guess who got a delivery?' Susie said, leaping from her chair and rushing to sweep Paige's office door open. 'Look.'

As if she could have missed it. A gargantuan bunch of flowers in a vase on her big glass desk—effusive, lush blooms of creams and greens—swamped everything else in the room. The feelings, fears, and flutterings smacking into one another as they went crazy inside her, Paige reached for the card with shaking fingers. Opened it.

The message was simple. Cryptic. And not from Gabe.

I owe you one, it read, signed *Nate Mackenzie*.

Gabe's business partner? What on earth would he be thanking her for—?

Oh, God. The one and only time they'd talked he'd asked for a favour. He'd wanted her to use her influence to get Gabe to stay.

A rush of warm, hopeful, luxuriant, dangerous feelings swarmed her, so fierce and scattered she hadn't a hope in hell of controlling them.

She shoved the card back into the envelope and said, 'Thanks, Susie.'

Susie bounded on her toes, clearly desperate to ask about the flowers, but it was as clear that her boss wasn't about to spill the juice. She shut the door quietly on her way out.

Paige turned the glossy white wooden blinds until they let in as little sunlight as possible, threw her jacket and scarf over the pewter stand in the corner, then slowly sat in her chair. She moved the mouse to bring her monitor to life, clicked on the memo icon on the screen and tried to start her day. But the ridiculous spray of flowers occupying the left side of her vision taunted her. She gave up and reached out and ran her fingers over a pale velvety petal.

Was Gabe staying? He hadn't said anything about it last night. And for him he'd said a lot. So she couldn't dare hope. She couldn't dare discount it either. Either way, the time had come for damage control. To protect herself, as she had done her whole life.

Of course the most sensible thing to do was end it now. She laughed so loud she expected Susie to come running. Who was she kidding? She no more had the wherewithal to end it now than to chop off her own leg. But it would end. Whether quick and painful, or slow and painful, these things always did.

Paige bent over until her head thunked on her desk.

If she had any hope of getting off this roller coaster with an ounce of self-respect, she had to do whatever it took to make sure Gabe never guessed how she felt. She was going to have to remind him what their relationship was all about: *not* dates and feelings and impossible hopes.

She only hoped it wasn't too late.

When Gabe got home that evening he felt as if he were walking on air. He and Nate had spent the better part of the day in Nate's office, laughing, reminiscing, ordering in take-out, while the rest of the office went bonkers. Turned out one of the nice things about being such a success was that they could pay other people to deal with the fallout.

The day only got better when he walked into his apartment to find Paige sitting on his kitchen bench, toying with his flamingo mobile-phone holder. Her long legs crossed at the knees and the setting sunlight slicing between the buildings, creating gold, pink, and hot orange streaks across her body. Her *naked* body.

'Evening,' she said, a slumberous smile playing about her gorgeous mouth. Then she pulled a strawberry from a bowl beside her and slid it between her lips. The ripe red fruit popping in her mouth before her tongue swept out to lick away the juice. 'Want some?'

Heat sliced through his body in a devastating wave and his feet forgot how to move. She was every Sam Spade fantasy any man had ever had but with one big difference. She was real. Flesh and blood. Soft skin and softer lips and— He was so hard so fast he couldn't think any more.

He dropped his laptop bag to the floor, and went to

her; the last truly coherent thought was that he ought to speak to Sam the Super about security.

He was so hot for her it should have been over in half a minute, but the second his lips met hers, he tasted strawberry on his tongue, absorbed the warmth in her soft bare skin sliding against his palms, something shifted. And the whole world became still.

His eyes found hers, looking to see if she felt it too, but the sun's rays shimmered too bright in all that liquid blue. He tucked her hair behind her ears, and as she sucked in a short, sharp breath he saw it. Desire, need, anticipation. And something a lot like awe. Hit with an emotional wallop he couldn't hope to decipher in his rigid state, he knew there was no way to tell her how she made him feel. He'd have to show her.

Even as he burned with an ache he could barely contain, he slid an arm beneath her knees, and carried her to his room, his eyes not leaving hers. She blinked fast. Her breaths coming hard. And clasped her hands together behind his neck.

He took her to his big bed and gently laid her down. Her pale skin glowing against the rich dark brown of his sheets, her blonde hair splayed around her beautiful face, her eyes, dark with passion, watching him hungrily. She looked... He wanted... He knew...

Hell.

He tore off his clothes. Too many layers, damnable Melbourne winter. Then naked, protected, he lowered himself over her, carefully. Her eyes not once leaving his, she reached to cup his head, and pulled him down to kiss her. Deeply, slowly, thoroughly.

When she wrapped one long leg around his backside and moaned softly into his mouth, any control he might have had slipped away. He pressed himself against her opening to find her more than ready, and he pushed into her in one smooth stroke.

Skin on skin. Heat on heat. The slip and slide of their bodies created the most perfect friction he'd ever felt. Their eyes remained locked on one another throughout as he buried himself so deep inside her he wasn't sure how he'd ever find his way back.

Her mouth opened on a gasp, the muscles of her neck straining, her eyes drifting closed as he felt her tighten, and tighten, and tighten. The most luxurious torture consumed him right as she came in his arms with a cry that echoed around the room. He peaked while she still convulsed around him, the pleasure slamming to the absolute outer reaches of his consciousness. The devastating pressure eased from his body in slow receding waves, until he was left feeling boneless. Bare.

He pulled out, and lay down beside her, cradling her into him, his arm holding her between her breasts, her beautiful backside pressed against his groin, her hair beneath his cheek. And it wasn't long before her breaths settled to the soft puffs of sleep.

As he lay there, more wide awake than he could ever remember feeling, the world outside slid back into his mind. He was keeping BonaVenture. Which meant working more closely alongside Nate. And not leaving any time soon.

Paige had never hidden the fact that she was perfectly happy for their affair to be a short-term thing.

And he'd been right there with her. His staying would change everything. One way or the other.

She shifted in her sleep, the underneath of her foot sliding along the top of his, her cheek rising to press against his lips before she settled deeper into his pillow.

He had to tell her. She needed to know. Not while his whole body still hummed from the after-effects of making love to her.

He'd lived by his gut for long enough now, he'd know when the time was right.

Paige came back to consciousness slowly. Her body felt so drugged with pleasure she could barely open her eyes. But when Gabe's scent curled beneath her tongue she remembered where she was. In his bed, covered in a big dark blanket, with a big hard man tucked right in behind her.

The big seduction scene she had planned had gone up in smoke the second she'd looked into Gabe's eyes and realised how much she hoped he was staying. And then when, with so much gentleness, he'd stroked her hair from her face, she'd forgotten everything but how he made her feel. Safe, adored, hot as the sun.

All the control she'd planned to take back had slipped through her fingers, and now she felt as if she'd been turned inside out and pulled apart and put back together again wrong. No, not *wrong* so much as differently.

She turned, his big heavy arm sliding across her breasts. She pushed a lock of dark hair away to get a better look at him as he slept. His long dark lashes rested peacefully against his swarthy cheeks. His nostrils flared with each breath. Fresh stubble shadowed his jaw.

A sigh shot past her lips, bringing with it a sense of inevitability.

She'd spent so much time convincing herself that the intensity of their affair had sprung from the situation, her desperation to get laid and quick, his brief stay in town. But in that quiet place, that quiet moment, in his big beautiful bed with its Gabe-shaped dint in the middle that sloped their bodies towards one another, she gave up trying.

She placed her hand over his heart and with her next breath in she let herself feel the surge of sensations blooming inside her. The pinch in her chest, the warmth in her belly, the way her lungs felt as if they couldn't get quite enough air any more—like spots of ink dropped into a pond, spreading from her centre in little ripples that crashed softly against her skin.

Gabe stirred, the muscles in his chest undulating, sending her hand rolling over the smooth hot skin as if it were riding the crest of a wave.

This. This man. This heat. This *feeling*. It seemed as if there ought to be one word to sum all of that up.

There was a word, she realised as the ripples headed back to her centre and joined in a warm, solid, beautiful ache in her heart. A word she'd spent her life shunning, mocking, fearing.

It was love. And it had been coming on for so long it wasn't even a shock.

What it was was amazing. Beautiful. Consuming. A miracle.

I love you, Gabe, she whispered inside her head. Then, spent, she snuggled under the blankets and fell back asleep.

Paige nibbled on her little fingernail, or what was left of it, and watched Mae's mouth move as she gushed over a pair of sky-high white boots at Bridge Road discount shoe shop. But she heard nothing but the thoughts swimming through her head.

That which she'd only begun to fathom the night before had grown wings and taken flight. She was head over heels, deep and true, in love with Gabe. She'd done things, admitted things, felt things with him she'd never imagined she'd ever do. She'd never been with a man who made her feel safe enough to dare. She wanted to be with him, the way normal people had relationships. She wanted him to stay.

She'd about convinced herself she wasn't a sucker.

Gabe liked her. He trusted her. He wanted her. She knew all that for sure. There was also the fact that she'd given him more than his fair chances to wipe his hands of her, and something had kept him coming back for more. Didn't all that mean what she wanted was possible, not the fantasy her mother had believed was real?

'What do you think?' Mae asked, jabbing her with a high heel, pain finally pulling her into the present.

'About?'

'These,' Mae said, wiggling the boots in Paige's face.

'For what purpose?'

Mae blinked at her. 'For... My... Wedding. Where

are you right now? 'Cause as sure as I'm getting married you're not here.'

Paige pulled her finger from her mouth. 'I'm here. All yours. Now, boots. Well…that depends. Is your theme sexy Christmas elf?'

Mae grimaced and put the shoes back. 'Even though your taste is totally boring, this has been fun!'

'Totally.' And it had been. Shopping with Mae—*only* Mae—was always fun.

Mae said, 'Doesn't it feel like weeks since we've been able to do this, just the two of us?'

Paige laughed, then realised by Mae's blank smile that she hadn't been kidding. It hadn't occurred to Mae that it felt like weeks because it had *been* weeks. Which was why Paige was gripped by this amazing, delicious, petrifying, confusing, churning emotion and had no idea how to tell her best friend.

Paige picked up a hot-pink sparkly sandal and checked the price. 'Lucky you've got this wedding stuff to organise or we'd never see each other.'

'You've been the busy one of late. You and lover boy. In fact you look exhausted. And I think you should tell me in intimate detail exactly how he exhausted you last.'

At the mere mention of Gabe, Paige came over all hot and squidgy. Ignoring Mae she ran her fingers along the suede fringing of an aqua cowboy boot. Then she looked around and wondered if they'd walked into a shop meant for drag queens. Or hookers.

Mae gave an exaggerated sigh. 'Fine, then answer me this—when's your sexy pirate setting sail?'

Paige slowly put the pink sparkly sandal back in place, lining it up neatly. 'Not sure.'

Mae snuck a bite of a secret chocolate bar she had stashed in her handbag, while skimming a glance at the shop assistant hovering nervously around the array of absurdly expensive shoes. 'But that's still his plan, right?'

'I really don't know,' Paige said as she turned the lurid green pump that had somehow ended up in her hand. There'd been no mention of leaving, or staying for that matter, when she'd headed off around dawn. Just a kiss so lush and deep her toes had curled so hard they'd cramped.

Mae swallowed slowly. 'You haven't thought to ask?'

'No,' Paige said, exasperated. 'I haven't.'

Because she was benevolently waiting for *him* to bring it up? Or because deep down below all the lovely, warm, excited feelings tumbling about inside the spin dryer that was her tummy, she wondered why he hadn't talked it over with her already? Because it changed everything? Or because it didn't make any difference?

'Wow,' Mae said on a slow release of breath.

Paige looked up, expecting Mae to be eyeballing some other crazy pair of wedding-inappropriate shoes.

But Mae watched her, eyes huge. 'You're a goner.'

Paige *pffted* with all her might and grabbed a pair of a tomato-red peep-toed ankle boots and sat on the black velvet ottoman in the middle of the store and toed off her comparatively conservative ballet flats.

'Look at you,' Mae said, sitting right next to her. 'All flushed and trembly with that faraway look in your eyes. I caught you humming earlier. Some old movie song I couldn't put my finger on. Sandra Dee—no, Doris Day! I think you've even put on a little weight.'

'What?' Paige said, hands going to her hips as she looked down at her thighs splayed on the seat. Mae was probably right there, considering what amounted to a doughnut addiction of Gabe's, and how much she'd come to appreciate the perfect pleasure of dough and warm icing right after sex.

'Careful,' Mae said. 'You might melt right here on the shop floor. And I don't think *la shop girl* over there is big on mess.'

Paige put the boots down and stared at her chocolate brown toenails. 'Look. Gabe and I are... We haven't... I mean, I *like* him. I may even— But I'm not sure if he's—' Suddenly the boutique felt claustrophobic. 'Maybe we should head to that place down the corner. It has two floors and an espresso machine.' Paige had her feet in her shoes and was out of the door and off down the dodgy Richmond footpath, breathing in great gulps of chilly air.

Mae caught up a half-block down, taking her by the arm. 'Paige, wait. Hon, this is me you're talking to. Your best bud. What's going on?'

Best bud? Paige thought, turning to look at her friend. The friend who had no clue how afraid she was in that moment. Afraid of loving Gabe. Afraid that he might not love her back. Afraid that so long as she got to have him she could live with that.

Mae looked back at her. Same wild red hair, same piercing green eyes. The same, but not. No longer all hers.

Finally the pressure built so hard and fast inside Paige there was nowhere for it to go but out. 'You know why it feels like for ever since we've done this? Because the only things we do without Clint nowadays are wedding-related expeditions on which he is not allowed to come.'

Mae took a moment to catch onto the change of subject, before the colour drained out of her face. 'No! *No*. It's not like that.'

Mae looked so mortified, Paige's resentment deflated like a pricked balloon. 'Don't worry about it. It's okay. I get it. Life goes on.'

Mae pulled her out of the stream of foot traffic until they huddled on the stoop of a dark doorway that apparently led to a Brazilian wax clinic. *Of all places*, Paige thought, promising to backhand Lady Fate the next time they caught up.

Mae said, 'You know that nothing's changed between *us*. I'll always be there for you.'

Paige's throat felt as if it was closing up. 'You won't. You're already not.'

Mae opened her mouth but nothing came out. Then she frowned down at her Doc Martens with their red tartan laces. And Paige thought if nothing had changed Mae would wear *them* on her wedding day, not some vision of what she thought Clint might like.

The anger that churned through her at that thought pushed her the final step. Paige said, 'The past few months have been hard for me, Mae. Like I can't seem to get a foothold any more. In the past I'd have found it at work but even that's not enough any more. I think *that's* why I bought the dress. To feel something other than lost. Then along came Gabe. He makes me feel like I've been found. God, that's petrifying. That I might actually *need* him in some way, *any* way...' She closed her eyes, all her foolish feelings hurtling against the inside of her head.

'Tell me about it,' Mae said, her voice dripping with irony.

Paige opened her eyes to squint at Mae. 'Don't. You and Clint make it look so easy it burns.'

Mae threw her hands in the air and swore so loud Paige flinched. 'God, I'm gonna have to come out and say it, aren't I?'

'What?'

Mae's chutzpah faltered for a hundredth of a second before she said in a rush, 'I cheated on Clint.'

Every ounce of blood in Paige's body made a dash for her feet. She pressed her back against the door, the cold glass keeping the uncomfortable heat rushing through her body from overwhelming her. '*When* did you—?'

She couldn't even say the word. Not after what Mae's dad had put her mum through all those years ago. Mae knew the hurt, and had repeated her dad's mistakes anyway. Paige felt panic rising in her throat. Was a failing like that in the blood? Could it not be helped?

'A while back,' Mae said.

'Does he know?'

'Yeah.' Mae started pacing. 'Dammit! He'll hate that I told you.'

'But why?'

'Because it's nobody's business but ours.'

Paige felt as if she'd been slapped. And the cold of

the day had nothing on the chill sealing her emotions. Her voice was cool as she said, 'I meant, why did you cheat.'

But Mae was in such a state, Paige wasn't sure she'd even been heard.

Finally Mae stopped pacing and looked down the street. She tucked her hair behind her ears only for the wind to whip it back out sideways again. 'I told you because you need to know that *no* relationship is perfect. Not even the ones that might seem all rosy on the outside. And sometimes relationships can be imperfect *and* still be special and magical. Clint and I know each other's weaknesses and love one another anyway. There's an amazing comfort in that. Like whatever comes our way we know we can handle it. Together.'

Paige suddenly had a raging headache. Thumbs at her temples, eyes squinting, she said, 'Look, do you mind if we do this another day?'

'Sure,' Mae said, sliding her hands into the pockets of her coat as she stared hard at her shoes. 'There's no rush. Besides, Clint might not even recognise me if I walked down the aisle in white heels.'

At that it all became too much. Without another word, Paige headed off down the street. Her feet felt numb. Her head a mess. Her stomach as if it were trying to turn itself inside out.

She heard Mae's voice trail after her. 'Tell him! Tell him how you feel, Paige. You'll only regret it if you don't. Believe me.'

Paige just kept on walking.

And with every footfall she knew Mae was right

about one thing. She couldn't hide her feelings any more. She had to tell Gabe how she felt.

Not because she'd regret it if she didn't but because he was a good man who always tried to do the right thing. She'd tell him because he needed to know how brilliant he was. She'd tell him because not telling was lying, and she never wanted to hurt him as Mae had hurt Clint.

And she'd tell him because if she ever had any chance of making a life for herself, one that wasn't defined by mistakes other people made, it was now.

ELEVEN

—

Wednesday evening Gabe and Nate leant their backs against the edge of the dark city bar, enjoying the glow of a celebratory thirty-year-old Scotch.

Gabe was exhausted after being in the office most of the past two days knocking out a new company charter with Nate. But a good exhausted. As if he were twenty-five again with the wind at his back and the world at his feet. Only for the first time in years he didn't have to be running across the globe to keep the feeling going.

He closed his eyes to the chatter of Aussie accents, easy laughter, and he let the glow of life in his home town settle over him. There were ghosts—of his parents, his gran, his deepest regret—and always would be. But despite all that, as cities went Melbourne was pretty perfect now he came to think about it. The food, the bars, the sports. Even the strong seasonal weather was kind of lovely so long as you were ready for it.

And then there was Paige.

His eyes flickered open and the crowd swam in front of his vision. Yet for all the hustle and bustle he could still feel the gentle sweep of her finger across his forehead, the curl of her soft hand on his chest, the heat of her skin imprinting upon him, the air scooting over his collarbone as she'd whispered the words, *'I love you, Gabe.'*

His gut clenched the same now, a couple of days after the fact, and no amount of shifting on his stool changed that. At the time he'd pretended to be asleep. Not to have heard. He'd told himself it had been the afterglow talking. He'd come pretty close to nirvana that night himself.

But as the Scotch eased into his blood and the good people of BonaVenture laughed and celebrated in front of him, easing from his shoulders the years of guilt and self-recrimination, there was no deep dark place inside him to hide that moment any more.

It hadn't been the afterglow. Paige was in love with him.

For a moment, a sliver of time, he let the idea find a way beneath his skin. He couldn't kid himself. A good portion of the appeal of sticking around was about her. Being with her hadn't been easy. Hell no. The woman was as stubborn as a mule, and could be a real pain in the ass, but it was her spirit that had hooked him, drawn him in, steadied him. It had been some time since he'd decided Paige Danforth was his karmic gift.

But he'd never imagined it to be more than a beautiful affair. He'd never imagined that she might either. It had only been a few days back that he'd realised she hadn't even invited him into her apartment. When he'd kicked himself for being more invested than she was.

And yet...

He breathed out long and slow.

It was all there if he let himself see it. He'd seen it in her eyes. Felt it in her touch. Knew it in the unguarded way she gave herself up to him every time they had sex. It had been so long since he'd been anywhere near that depth of feeling he hadn't recognised that a gorgeous, seductive, testing dish of a woman *loved* him. The truth of it filled him like a wave of—

'Oh, and the nanotechnology deal fell through,' Nate said.

'I'm sorry?' Gabe said, blinking back into the light as the wave of sensation turned out to be a prickle of sweat all over his body.

Nate motioned to the waiter dashing past to bring them both another of the same.

'Think hard,' Nate said. 'You spent a few days in Sydney the other week—'

Gabe ignored the drink the barman slid beside his elbow. 'Yeah yeah yeah. What I don't think I heard right was that I didn't land it.'

'They went another way. Don't sweat it.'

Don't sweat it? Too damn late. The prickles of sweat now felt like a million tiny little needles calling for his blood. Gabe turned on his stool to face the back of the bar, elbows landing on the sticky surface, fingers covering his mouth as he stared unseeingly into the dark mirror.

He didn't *not* land deals. Ever. He was the rainmaker. Failure was not in his vocabulary. It was *the* talent he brought to the table. The only time it had deserted him had been when he'd been distracted by real life—

Paige. Half the time away he'd spent thinking about Paige. The other half he'd been trying not to think about her. He'd called in the work, hadn't he? Because he'd thought it parochial and easy. And because he'd practically had a hard-on all week.

Dammit. He sat forward and rubbed his hands over his eyes.

From the moment Paige had tried to jam his fingers in the lift door, he'd known she was a train-wreck in the making. Yet he'd jumped on board because being with her had been intoxicating. For a man who hadn't felt much of anything in a long time the rush had been impossible to resist.

He'd had an excuse the first time he'd let a beautiful blonde take his eye off the ball. This time he had none. He'd clearly learned nothing since he'd been gone. And the realisation made him feel ten different kinds of reckless.

The ride had been something, but it was time to get off. He'd done what he'd come to Melbourne to do and now it was time to go. The prickles eased the moment he made the decision, and he had to believe that meant something, as his gut was the only moral compass he had left.

His hand found the drink, the ice clinking gently against the glass. And as he lifted it to his mouth he caught his reflection. Distorted by rows of spirit bottles lined up along the dark mirror behind the bar, he recognised his father's jaw, his mother's dark hair, his gran's eyes.

And his own big fat lie.

Moral compass, my ass. He'd been desperate for an excuse to jump ship the second Paige had whispered those four soft words into the darkness. Because they'd tugged hard at something inside him. Something he'd thought lost. Something he'd trusted would stay that way.

Love wasn't something he sought or wanted in his life. All love meant to him was loss.

His memories of his parents were rare, and even then they'd flicker into his mind and fade as fast, leaving a hollow ache in their place. His memories of his gran went deeper. Her toughness and substance and faith had given him the foundation from which he'd built his life. And when she'd died he'd lost his way.

This damn city, he thought. There were too many ghosts after all. He knew he'd stayed away for good reason. This time he wouldn't ever let himself forget.

Not caring to look himself in the eye any longer, he spun back around.

In the end it really didn't matter why. His decision was made. And it was for the best.

Gabe told himself it was for the best a hundred times between then and when he knocked on Paige's apartment door.

When she opened up music twanged in the background. It faded to a blur as he took in the sight of her: bare feet, hair pulled back into a messy ponytail, faded pink T-shirt stretched across her breasts, old jeans barely clinging to her hips revealing a sliver of flat stomach. Without her usual high heels and eclectic layers she seemed smaller. Softer. Sweet as all hell.

So he told himself again.

'Come in, come in,' she said, her voice breathless, her smile hesitant. But then she tipped up onto her toes and slid her arms around his neck. Pressed her body against his. And let out a long sigh.

And before he even knew what he was doing he slid his arms around her waist and held her tight. Her scent, her taste, her heat infusing him till his blood fizzed with it.

So he told himself *again*.

'You look tired,' she said as she sank back on her heels. She licked something off her fingers as she padded deeper into the kitchen. Something sweet if the warm scents coming at him from her apartment were anything to go by. Sweet because she knew that was how he liked it.

When she glanced back over her shoulder, her chin tilted down, her finger caught between her teeth, her eyes smiling, her feelings for him were so transparent it hurt. Deep behind his ribs.

And he knew he'd never have to tell himself again.

When she realised he hadn't moved, she spun on her toes and faced him, her forehead creased into a frown. 'Something up?'

'I'm leaving.' There, whip off the Band-Aid fast. Better for her. Better for him.

Her finger remained in her mouth a beat before it slowly slid free. Frown still in place, she reached for a tea towel and slid it through her fingers. 'Where to this time?'

He didn't have an answer. That afternoon he'd scoured his emails and found a couple of early leads in Paris and Brussels. Another in Salt Lake City. But he didn't have a flight booked. He'd take whichever came first and research from there.

Her eyes slid past him and landed on his bags out in the hall—the same bags he'd arrived with weeks before. 'You're leaving? As in *leaving*.'

He nodded. Jaw clenched against the dawning realisation in her eyes. He could see her fighting it. Fighting the inevitability they'd both selfishly ignored.

'But I thought... I mean, aren't you...?' She shook her head, as if trying to clear out the cobwebs. 'When will you be back?'

'Not sure. Depends on the work.'

Her eyebrows slowly lifted as if she wasn't buying that one for a second. 'From what I heard you're the boss. Seems a man in that position can make his own hours.'

'That's not the way I operate. Never has been.'

The tea towel gripped tight about her hands, she placed her fists on one hip. 'Right. Then maybe you can answer this one. How long were you gone last time you ran away?'

'A while,' he said, before realising he hadn't denied he was running.

'Weeks. Months. Years?'

'About that.'

She nodded, hurt, anger, and possibly worst of all resignation twisting her lovely features. She slowly uncurled the tea towel from its death grip and placed it on the bench. 'Is this where you assure me we can take up where we left off when you next swing through town?'

He gritted his teeth against the glimmer of hope in her big blue eyes that belied the sarcasm in her tone. He'd never imagined it would be this hard to do the right thing. But he could do it. If only because he knew if he gave an inch he'd be *her* anchor, only so much as he'd be holding her back when she deserved to be happy. Happy with someone who knew how to be happy with her.

When he said nothing, the glimmer of hope snuffed out. If she could have turned him to ice with a look, he'd have been a frozen solid on the spot. 'Wow. I can't believe I hoped you'd say yes. How close I came to being that woman. The one who accepts the dregs if that's all she can get from the man she—'

She swallowed back the next word, and Gabe was so thankful he hated himself.

Her chin hitched north as she looked him right in the eye and promised, 'I'll *never* be her.'

All warmth, and sweetness, and vulnerability had fled, locked behind an ice-cool façade. The façade she showed other men. The façade she'd let down for him. It should have made it easier, the distance she was putting between them, instead he wanted her to fight back. To let loose a storm of angry heat in his direction.

But if cool was what she needed, then cool she'd get. 'Atta girl.'

A flicker of heat glinted within the wall of ice blue and he pressed his feet into the floor. 'So if this is it, if this is such a simple goodbye for you, why are you even here? Why tell me to my face?'

She had him there. But he couldn't think up an answer that made any sense. So he went with the incontrovertible, 'This was only ever going to be short term. You know that.'

'You choose now to remember that? You, the man who asked *me* on a date. The man whose best friend sent me flowers as he thought it was because of me that he was—' She shook her head again, before it drooped as if she no longer had the strength to hold it up.

Dammit. Gabe took a step inside her kitchen until he was close enough to touch. To catch her scent above the scent of baking; far sweeter than any doughnut, or anything else he'd ever known. 'Paige, you are an amazing woman—'

'Stop. Right there.'

'No.'

She flinched at his tone. Then slowly looked up. The deep sadness and hurt in her eyes killing him. But his decision was made. And it wasn't about what he wanted. It was about what he *had* to do.

He reached out and tucked a stray strand of soft blonde hair behind her ear. 'It's been...' *Dazzling. Tender. Once in a lifetime.* 'A hell of a ride.'

She swallowed. Her eyes flicking between his as if she still couldn't quite believe it. As if she might yet wake up and find it was all a bad dream.

He must have moved towards her because suddenly she was sinking into him with a sigh, her hands splayed out across his back, her head against his chest.

He rested his chin on her head, closed his eyes, and told himself *this* was shoring up his karmic balance. And maybe from that point on he could truly start his life afresh.

With an effort greater than himself he pulled away. 'Goodbye, Paige.'

She wrapped her arms around herself and nibbled at her heavenly bottom lip, refusing to say goodbye.

Gabe could barely feel his feet as he walked out of her door. He lifted his bags to his shoulder and pressed the button for the lift. The door opened instantly, he stepped inside. He didn't even get a chance to look back, or not, as the lift door practically bit his backside as it snapped shut behind him and he was going down before he'd even picked a floor.

Paige went the only place she could think that would stop her from shattering into a thousand pieces. To Mae. So when Clint opened the door to his apartment he couldn't have looked more surprised than she felt. Somehow she'd forgotten he even existed. What a mess.

'Hey, Paige,' Clint said, looking at her chin rather than her eyes, meaning she must have looked an absolute treat. 'Ah-h, Mae's not here.'

'Right.' She sniffed, rubbing at the sore spot under her ribs where it felt as if a chopstick had been jammed for good. 'Can I come in anyway?'

He glanced inside to where the sports channel blared on the TV. 'There's a replay of the Pies game. I was kinda looking forward to unbuttoning my jeans and burping out loud.'

The guy was a human Labrador; it simply wasn't in him to be unkind. So she knew his hesitation could only mean one thing. He knew that she knew that Mae had cheated. But whatever he saw in her face in the end he pushed the front door open and waved her under his arm.

Five minutes later, Paige sat curled up on Clint's faded old tartan couch, a musty-smelling throw tucked around her, a cup of hot chocolate warming her palms as he told his side of Mae's story, which turned out to be the best possible way she could have distracted herself from her own mess of a love life. From the knowledge she'd been moments from telling Gabe she loved him, right before he'd summarily dumped her.

'We'd been going out for about two months when I walked into a party to find her with her tongue down my friend's throat, his hands making a joke of her top.'

'Why?' Paige asked, even while she wasn't sure she wanted to know why Mae had done it, or why Clint had forgiven her. Because if they couldn't get this love thing right what hope was there for anyone?

Clint sat forward, the fire flickering in the old grate creating shadows across his kind face. 'You grow up assuming you'll find the one, but as you get older you realise it's as rare as finding a bar of gold bullion in your cornflakes. Then one day you walk into the same bar you've been in a hundred times before and there she is.'

It seemed too easy to say love conquered all. And too hard all at the same time. 'But she *cheated* on you. With a *friend*. How could that not be game over?'

He twirled his beer in both hands. 'Of course she

picked a friend. Love is a scary thing, and she loved me too much already to walk away.'

Paige shook her head, trying to follow the anti-logic, even while it made absolute sense in a way that surprised her to her very roots. 'Are you guys still friends? You and the guy?'

Clint's eyebrows all but disappeared into his tidy crew cut. 'I decked the guy. Broke his nose. It's only that he felt like a right git for what he'd done that he didn't press charges. A man's gotta do what a man's gotta do for the woman he loves.'

The commentators on the screen suddenly went wild and Paige realised Clint was being abnormally quiet considering the Magpies had scored a ripper goal. She glanced across to find him staring into the middle distance, his eyes glassy, the fingers of his right hand flexing, as though sense memory made them feel the pain of the strike. And only then did she notice the knuckles of his other hand had turned white on his beer.

'Aren't *you* scared?'

'Of what exactly?' Clint asked.

'It not working out? Her leaving? Her cheating again? Her not loving you as much as you love her?'

'Sure. I have my moments. But they pass. And they're worth it. Because *she's* worth it.'

The clench in Paige's stomach was the very definition of bittersweet. 'She's really getting married, isn't she?'

Clint could have laughed. She wouldn't have blamed him. But the sweetheart reached over, wrapped a big brotherly hand around her head, and tucked it into his shoulder. And he sat there and let her tears soak into his sweatshirt. Without judgment or advice. Just acceptance.

It seemed he understood, way more than she even had herself, that she was grieving. Had been since the moment she'd seen that ring on Mae's finger. It had meant the end of the most important, strong, invincible relationship of her life.

What she hadn't realised was that it could be the beginning of another. She pulled back. Looked into Clint's kind hazel eyes. If Mae was the closest thing she had to a sister, then that made Clint family too.

She gave him a watery smile. And with a wink he lifted his beer in a salute and served himself a piece of pizza that looked as if it had cooled and congealed many hours before, before pressing the volume button on the remote.

Paige breathed deep through her nose and pulled the blanket up under her chin, knowing he'd be gone to her now for a good bit unless she had something derogatory to say about the umpires.

She grabbed a piece of cold pizza and noticed that the pizza box sat alongside myriad mug rings and a corner of a magazine page that had been stuck there years before by something sticky. Elsewhere, fishing rods poked out of the tall pot in the corner. A bike with muddy wheels leant against the wall in the entrance.

She was surprised Mae hadn't made more of a mark, filling the place with wild cushions and a top of the line espresso machine. Even Paige's place still had touches of Mae about it. It seemed Clint was a man who knew himself. Who knew exactly how far he was able to be pushed. And how far he'd go in the name of love.

Paige's heart clenched again, but left alone with her thoughts this time there was no fighting it. She had to ride the pain. To own it. To learn from it. And to imagine how it would feel to take Mae by the collar and shake her till her brain rattled for nearly screwing things up with this amazing guy.

When prickles shot down her legs, warning her if she'd waited another five minutes she'd likely have lost all feeling in them, she untucked them. Right as the front door creaked, groaned, and snapped open, and Mae bustled through the door carrying Chinese food and more beer.

'And there she is,' Clint said. 'The woman I love.'

When Mae saw Paige sitting on her couch, beside her fiancé, snuggled under an afghan, she baulked. Paled. Her expression hovering somewhere between a pained smile and a frown.

Paige threw the blanket aside and leaned over and gave Clint a kiss. 'Be good to her or I'll rip off your boy bits and feed them to my ferret.'

'You don't have a ferret.'

'I'll get one.'

Clint smiled. Sweet man. Strong man. Good man. Good enough for her Mae.

Paige stood up, padded over to Mae on wobbly legs. Mae looked as if she'd yet to take a breath. Until Paige reached out and enveloped her in a great big bear hug. With a whimper Mae pressed back with all her might, her version of a hug considering her arms were full.

'You look like crap,' Mae said.

'Feel like it too. I'll tell you about it later, I promise.'

'Chinese is getting cold!' Clint called out.

Mae sniffed. 'Handle it!'

'All righty, then,' said Clint.

Paige laughed, amazing considering the day she'd had. But even while her heart felt as if it had been pounded with a meat hammer, there was enough left to feel happy for Mae. Happy her friend had found the most important, strong, invincible relationship of *her* life.

To Mae she said, 'Be good to him.'

Mae's eyes shifted sideways, landed on her fiancé, who was flapping a hand at the TV, his voice rising by the second, backside halfway off the couch, willing his team forward from his position at wing-via-couch. With a sigh she said, 'Always and for ever.'

Then Mae all but ran to the couch, snuggled in under her fiancé's waiting arm.

The pain beneath Paige's ribs eased a tiny little bit, and she managed to swallow back the tears that had started—happy for them, devastated for herself—before she closed the door behind her.

As she walked along the Richmond back streets to the tram stop, the icy winter wind snuck through her clothes, but she shoved her hands deep into the pockets of her warm jacket and kept walking, Clint's words playing through her mind on a loop.

A man's gotta do what a man's gotta do for the woman he loves.

She'd thought Gabe cared. Even with her limited experience she'd been near certain that he felt the same way. Had she been so completely wrong?

If all he'd wanted was meaningless sex, he could have kept her on a string. And she might have let him. It could have gone on that way for months. Years. But he hadn't. He'd made a clean break, giving up a sure thing to save her from herself.

While she'd been not nearly so self-sacrificing. She'd kept Gabe at a distance from the beginning. She'd made it all about sex while he'd been the one to suggest a date. She'd never told Mae about him, while he'd told Nate about her. She'd never made any effort to let him into her life, while he'd opened his apartment to her on day one.

Even at the last she'd not told him how she felt. Never told him she wanted him to stay.

No wonder he'd found it so easy to walk away. Because she'd stood there and let him.

TWELVE

Gabe leant back in the wrought-iron chair in the outdoor café at the edge of St Mark's square, his unfocused gaze touching on huddles of wide-eyed tourists gawping at the architecture, and lean, young, dark-haired Venetian men checking out the female tourists.

Pigeons cooed and fluttered across his vision. He downed the remnants of his espresso, then went back to the dozen new emails from different departments back at BonaVenture HQ: Research, Accounts, PR.

Nate, who'd seemed not all that surprised when he'd left, but had also made him swear in blood he'd be gone no longer than a month, had also made him promise to use BonaVenture's extensive resources rather than try to do everything on his own. Thankfully the guy had an eye for talent because even while Gabe was sure he was halfway to landing the deal, and beating out four other mobs vying for the chance, his level of care didn't amount to a hill of beans.

They'd land it or they wouldn't. And life would, in fact, go on.

What had been keeping him up nights was that he found it near impossible to imagine what kind of life that might be.

Before closing his email, he scrolled down, in case he'd missed any messages. But no. No phone messages missed either. Not the one he was hoping for, anyway.

The day he'd arrived in Venice he'd wandered the meandering streets to get on local time, and had come to a halt at the sight of a pair of battered pink lawn flamingos leaning at an odd angle amongst the junk in the dusty window of a bric-a-brac shop. He'd taken a photo on his phone and messaged it to Paige.

A peace offering, he'd told himself as he'd pressed Send, because he wished he'd handled the dissolution of their affair with more style. But that was hogwash. He'd wanted to know she was thinking about him, even if for a moment. Even if it was to consider him pond scum. Because he thought about her constantly.

He knew he'd done the right thing in making a clean break, and yet he didn't feel righteous. He felt...lonesome.

Gabe slammed his laptop shut, slid it into his satchel, and hooked the strap over his head. He slid his sunglasses onto his face and picked a random corner of the square and set to getting lost in the bewildering twisting cobbled alleyways of Venice once again. Knowing he could never truly be lost. All paths led to the water.

Where Melbourne was full of white noise—Nate, BonaVenture, his parents, his gran, Lydia—every cor-

ner turned compounding his alienation, Venice held
no memories for him as yet. As such it was quiet. So
quiet he could no longer ignore the voices in his head.

He'd convinced himself he'd left Paige so he'd never
have to lose her, thus losing her anyway. At a distance
that made about as much sense as cutting off his toes
when the temperature dropped in case of possible future frostbite. And under the quiet blue Italian sky it
had become all too clear: all his adult life he'd avoided
intimacy, love, contentment because he felt he hadn't
earned it.

Guilt had a way of twisting a person and he'd been
twisted for so long he couldn't remember what it was
like to be simple and straight up and down. But until
he'd heard Paige's gutsy confession in that soft, sweet,
sure voice, he'd never known what twisted really felt
like.

He pulled up short of skittling a clump of tourists
leaning over a bridge watching a gondolier, straw hat
at a rakish angle, slide his boat artfully along the canal
below, 'O Sole Mio' tripping from his practised lips,
and sending all the girls into giggling swoons.

The song tickled at the corner of his memory—the
cab-ride through water-washed Melbourne the night
of their one and only date. He'd fought for Paige then.
As the water twinkled up at him he began to understand why. He'd been falling for her already, and, even
while he'd been scrambling to regain traction on his
old life, his instincts had told him to stick with her
instead.

He grumbled, 'Excuse me,' and bodily lifted a kid

out of the way so as to get past. To keep moving. Round and round in circles, twisty, like a rat in a maze.

Soon enough, he hit the water again and the nefarious scent of the canal was enough to have him turning straight up the next alley he found. This one dark, dank, narrowing, as close to being lost in the city as he could hope to be. He walked till sweat gathered beneath his armpits and his bag made his shoulder ache. Until a patch of sunshine filtered through the precariously inclining buildings to either side.

There he stopped. Tilting his face to the warmth. And with every deep breath out he let the quiet in. As everything fell away, every sliver of guilt, and sadness, and regret, the vacant spaces began to fill. With sunshine, with warmth, with hope. And with Paige. Her scent, her skin, her smile, her eyes, her tenacity and her temper. And that one night, wrapped around him in the warmth of his bed, when she had whispered that she loved him.

Something dazzling blinded him—a flash of sunshine, a reflection off water somewhere. And when he blinked the ground beneath his feet shifted so fast he held out his arms to get his balance.

Sucking in air, he knew the groundswell had nothing to do with the fact that the only things keeping the entire city from falling into the sea were thousands of wet sticks. It was vertigo. Paige-induced vertigo. She made his heart race, and his blood rush, and kept him more than a little off balance. And while it wasn't easy, and nothing was guaranteed, *that*, that energy, that exhilaration, that acute reminder that he was alive, was the exact flash of fire, of brilliance, he'd spent his whole life chasing.

Breathing deep, the impossible scent of orange so strong in his nostrils even the pervasive scent of the Venetian waterways didn't make a dent, he shielded his eyes as he looked up at the pale clear sky and attempted to figure out where he was.

And which direction he had to go to get home.

Paige did a last-minute check on the details of the Brazil recce trip.

Everything was in place—the hotel, the permission to use the beach, the local suppliers, the photographer. Once she was happy everything was right to go, she checked she had her passport, left a message on Sam the Super's phone that she'd be away—for whatever that was worth. Then she locked her apartment door and slid the key into an envelope to leave in Mrs Addable's mail box so her upstairs neighbour could water her plants.

She pressed the down arrow outside the lift and watched the number display above the lift, trying her best to stamp down her rising impatience. But she wanted to get on that plane as soon as humanly possible. She was so tense, when the lift binged almost instantly, she flinched. And when the lift doors slid open—

Her heart skipped a beat.

Because inside the lift, in leather and soft denim and huge scuffed boots, looking exactly as big, and dark, and dangerous as the day they'd first met was—

'Gabe?'

'Morning, Paige.'

The deep rumbling voice clinched it, vibrating down her spine, searing her to the spot so that she couldn't move, and filling her up with so much heartache she could barely contain it.

Because he'd left without even a backward glance. *Protect yourself!* a familiar old voice yelled in the back of her head. But as she drank him in, his dark soulful eyes, his big broad shoulders, his knee-melting scent, she told the voice to sod off.

She was done preparing for the worst. It felt a whole lot better hoping for the best. And if there was even a remote chance she could have what Mae and Clint had, then she needed to be ready for it. Open to it. Even if it meant having her heart broken all over again. The risk was worth it. Gabe was worth it.

'I was hoping to catch you before you headed into work,' he said, all smooth and nonchalant, as if he weren't meant to be on the other side of the world.

Work? As if she'd be let through the Ménage à Moi doors in her airplane uniform of beanie, ten-year-old electric-blue stretchy pants, faded Bon Temps football T-shirt, blazer, fluffy socks and Mae's old Docs.

And then she realised. He hadn't noticed her clothes. Hadn't even noticed the huge blood-red suitcase at her feet. His eyes hadn't once left hers. He'd only seen *her*. Just as he had that first morning in the lift when she'd been carrying a garment bag bright enough to be seen from the moon. And every day since. Bar, of course, the days since he'd told her she was amazing and left.

'What are you doing here?' she asked, heart trying

its dandiest to be hopeful, but it was struggling with the new skill. 'You're meant to be in Venice.'

His eyebrow rose, and she realised belatedly she'd given away that she'd found out where he was. 'I am,' he said. 'I was. Now I'm not. Seems I have a whole staff I can get to do the hard yards for me, leaving me to swoop in at the last and look brilliant.'

'Lucky you.' When Paige realised she was gripping the handle of her suitcase so hard the tops of her fingers were becoming numb, she eased off. 'I'm not heading into work, but you did just catch me. I'm meant to be heading to Brazil.'

With what seemed like considerable effort, Gabe dragged his eyes from hers long enough to take in her beanie, her take-no-prisoners boots, her massive red bag. 'Brazil? The catalogue. You won them over. Well done you. You'll love it. What time's your flight?' Even as he congratulated her he moved to the front of the lift, both hands gripping the doors, as if blocking her way.

'I said I'm *meant* to be heading to Brazil.'

His dark eyes slid back to hers. And the twin flints of heat and hope lighting their dark depths had her heart thumpety thumping against her ribs so hard she had to check to make sure her T-shirt wasn't dancing in time.

'Meaning you're not.'

'Not. I too have underlings and sent them in my stead.'

His nostrils flared as he breathed deep. As he considered the connotations of what she'd said. As he leaned an inch out into the hall.

'Look at us,' he rumbled, 'delegating.' And look he did, all the way down her legs and back up again with such concentration she felt every touch of his gaze like a caress. 'Frees up the spare time, I find.'

'Whatever will we do with it?'

'Come here,' he said, with a tilt of his chin, moving his big body aside, 'and I'll give you some ideas.'

Paige didn't have to be asked twice. She shoved her suitcase against her front door, tossing her handbag and key in the same general direction, then practically leapt into the lift.

Once inside, she scooted to the back before she glanced up at him, his breadth blocking out the light, making the room feel so tight with him in it. And, God, he smelled good. Of fresh air, and clean cotton, and spice, and soap, and every good manly thing.

The lift doors might have closed at that point. Or they might not. Paige was trying too hard to find some kind of rhythm in her breath to notice much of anything but the man in her sights. The man moving slowly her way.

When he got close enough she had to look up to see him, she took a step back, but he just moved closer still. So close her fingers itched with the effort not to slide her hand up the soft cotton of his T-shirt, scrunching the fabric into her hands, revealing all that hot male skin as she went. To run across his over-long stubble. To smooth out the new creases across his brow. He looked tired.

'Long flight?' she asked.

'Long week,' he said, his eyes roving over her face. Then, as they landed on her eyes, 'Longest of my life.'

He moved closer. Close enough she could just make out the rim of dark brown around his bottomless black pupils. 'If you're not going to Brazil, where are you going?'

Here goes, she thought. *No going back from here.* 'I'm going to Venice.'

'Are you now?' he rumbled, his voice like velvet as he kept on coming.

She rocked back on her heels till her shoulders hit the lift wall. And Gabe couldn't be any closer without touching her. So touch her he did, his big hand sliding around her waist to settle in the sweet spot of her lower back, his heat wrapping around her like a blanket.

With a sigh she felt to the bottoms of her feet, Paige slid her hands up his arms to curl around his big leather-clad biceps. 'I hear it's lovely this time of year.'

'It rains this time of year. Thunderstorms like you wouldn't believe.'

Had he pressed closer still? She could feel his heart thundering against her chest and one hard thigh nudged between hers. Her eyes fluttered closed and she had to force them to open back up again. 'Is that why you're back? Fear of storms to go with your fear of small spaces.'

He stilled as humour flared in his dreamy dark eyes. Until they came over so serious her chest began to ache in the most beautiful way. He shook his head. 'Clear skies as far as the eye could see.'

'Oh.' She licked her lips. Needing to know, needing to hear him say it. And looking into his face, so beautiful, so close after all those nights when it had been so far, she found the courage to ask, 'So why are you back?'

His dark eyes flickered between hers, and after what felt like for ever, he said, 'I have something for you.'

He tilted sideways and her body followed his like metal shavings to a magnet. Then she saw the bulky item wrapped in newspaper leaning next to her against the wall of the lift and she near leapt out of her skin. It came near to her shoulders, and she hadn't even seen it.

From the second the lift doors had opened she'd only seen him.

He grabbed the package and held it out to her. 'For you.'

She took it, peeling away the Italian newspaper it had been hastily wrapped in. The guy really hadn't a clue about garnish. And she loved him all the more for trying.

A black eye peeked out of the newspaper. Then a pink head. A darker pink beak. Two beaks. The newspaper fell to her feet with a scrunch and a shuffle and she was left holding two bruised and battered vintage flamingo lawn ornaments, pink paint worn away in places, their necks curved into a heart as they touched beaks.

Gabe might not have known a thing about garnish but he knew plenty about her. So much so her heart was lodged so far up into her throat she didn't know what to say.

'They're the ones from the photo,' he explained.

She sniffed as discreetly as possible and willed away the tears burning the backs of her eyes. 'What photo?'

'The one I texted to you.'

Her hand went to her phone in the back pocket of her stretchy-pants, only to remember it was in her handbag. Her bag she'd left in the hallway, while the lift was sailing past goodness knew what floor. She was about to find out how trustworthy her neighbours were.

'That? I thought you'd accidentally sent it to the wrong person.' And that fate could be a cruel cow at times.

'But...isn't that why you were coming to Venice?'

Suddenly big bad Gabe Hamilton looked unsure. He'd come all the way from Venice to bring her a couple of used flamingos and he'd done so without any guarantee of what he might find. If she'd thought she couldn't have loved him more than she did after seeing his gift, she'd been dead wrong. And now was the time to tell him.

But she'd planned to spend the next twenty-four hours' travelling to come up with the right thing to say. So that he'd hear her. So that he'd believe.

Paige swore inelegantly as she planted her feet and her hands flew out to her sides as the lift shuddered and the lights flickered to low. By the cessation of vibration through her legs she realised the lift had stopped. Her eyes cut to Gabe, to find his hand on the emergency button. Gabe who, no matter how he might try to deny it, was at least a little claustrophobic.

He took the flamingos from her hand and leant them against the wall, then grabbed a hank of hair poking out from under her beanie and gave it a tug. 'You know why I'm back, Paige.'

When his hands moved to brush her neck, to run over her shoulders, his thumbs tracing the edges of her breasts before his long fingers curled beneath her blazer and around her waist, Paige's whole body pulsed so hard she wrapped her fingers around the lapels of his thick leather jacket to keep herself from collapsing in a heap.

'I'd like to think so,' she said, 'but I'm not averse to hearing you say it.'

Humour flared in his eyes again. Humour and heat. Then he leant his forehead against hers. 'I'm back,' he rumbled in his deep delicious voice, 'because you love me.'

Paige hiccuped a half-sob half-laugh. Then she croaked, 'Excuse me?' her hand flying to her throat, but Gabe caught it, bringing her knuckles to his lips. His eyes closing as he breathed deep, drinking her in.

'You love me,' he said. He turned her hand to press his lips to the leaping pulse inside her wrist. 'You told me so. Soft and warm and sated in my bed.'

'I didn't say that out loud! Did I?'

'You did. I can all but feel your breath whispering against my cheek even now.'

Paige's spare hand flew to her own burning hot cheek. He knew she loved him. And he was still standing there, kissing the tips of her fingers. 'You knew, and yet you—' *Left.*

Gabe placed her hand over his heart, and then cradled her cheeks to make sure she was looking him right in the eye as he said, 'I knew and I found it hard to believe. Right up until I found it impossible not to believe.'

Gabe didn't make it any easier for her to get a grip on what was happening when he began raining soft warm kisses across her forehead, below her eyes, at the corners of her mouth. Then with a groan he swept his hands to take possessive rights on her backside, and he nuzzled her neck, warm air scooting across the sweet spot below her ear.

His voice vibrated through her as he said, 'I've spent every day since I've known you convincing myself it was all happening too fast to be real. That you were too good to be true. That I needed more time to be sure.'

The old Paige would have said, *Amen* to that. But the new and improved Paige was falling deeper and deeper into a blood haze and she flipped his leather jacket out of the way so she could find a backside to hold. So that she could press her hips into his. To tilt her head to give him all the access to her sweet spots he wanted. 'And now?'

'It only took ten thousand miles and trying to live a life I'd outgrown to realise when it comes to you, Paige Danforth, there's no such thing as too fast.' Gabe lifted his head, his eyes dark with desire. 'I'm in love with you, Paige. And I'm ready for you to love me right on back.'

That was all Paige needed to hear. She ran the back of her hand along his cheek, over his week-old stubble, then threaded her fingers through his dark hair and pulled his head to hers. A groan left his mouth as their lips met and she melted into him, heat on heat, hands everywhere as they couldn't get close enough.

He smelled so good, felt so strong, her limbs were so loose, her blood on fire, her heart full to bursting. *This* was what she'd worked so hard to avoid? Never again.

She dragged herself from the fog of his kiss, and, while she could have watched him looking hungrily at her lips for ever, she waited till his eyes left her mouth to look into hers to say, 'I love you more than you can know.'

'I reckon you love me exactly as much as I know.'

Paige pressed onto her toes and kissed him again. Only this time it was soft, lingering, searching, finding. A kiss that had found its home. A tear ran down her cheek as emotion too great to hold back overwhelmed her.

Gabe pulled back, licking her tear from his lips, and wiped a gentle knuckle down the trail. 'Now that we've got that all sorted out, you weren't busy, were you?'

Paige laughed, and thought of the suitcase that was hopefully still outside her apartment. 'Nothing pressing.'

'Good, because I'm in the mind to buy a suit and thought you might be the girl to help me pick one out.'

'A suit? I've never seen you wear a suit. Not once.'

'Turns out I need the right inducement.'

'Such as?'

'I'm not sure my leather jacket quite goes with that dress of yours. The white one with all the beads—'

'Pearls,' Paige corrected, even as her blood began to rush so fast through her system she thought she might be about to faint.

'Hmm?'

'They're natural freshwater pearls. Just saying.'

His mouth kicked up into the beginnings of a smile.
A flash of teeth. A crinkling of his eyes. A mere hint of
the smile that had got her into this in the first place
and she had to swallow down the flood of saliva that
poured into her mouth.

'Right,' he said. 'The way I see it, if you hadn't
bought the dress with the *pearls* you wouldn't have
wished for me. If I hadn't caught you in the dress,
hadn't been forced to rid you of it like a groom on his
wedding night, I might never have been snapped out
of my self-delusion that I'd never want to do it for
real. That dress came with a little bit of fairy dust,
methinks. Only fair I get me a suit to match. You in?'

Paige tried to think. She really did. But the thought
of Gabe fresh shaven, in morning grey, top hat, tails,
pearl buttons on the waistcoat and a matching pale
cream cummerbund was so ridiculous a picture she
laughed out loud.

'Something funny about the idea of you marrying
me, Miss Danforth?'

Her laughter stopped quick smart as Gabe slid down
onto his knee, just one knee, and lifted her top to place
a kiss on her belly. She slid her fingers into his long
thick hair and shook her head. Then, her own knees
giving way, she sat on his.

'You want to marry me?'

'You don't think I came all the way back here carrying a pair of love-locked flamingos on a whim, do you?
You're it. You're mine. I'm done. And I'm already looking forward to seeing the faces of your fan club as they
watch you walk down the aisle.'

Not having a clue as to what he was talking about,

Paige shook her head. 'I know you, Gabe. You won't see a single person in the crowd but me.'

'True. So you're in?'

'All the way in.' She held up a finger when his smile grew. 'On one condition. I don't want you wearing a suit for me. I love you just the way you are.'

'Yeah,' he said, sliding her beanie off her head and scrunching it behind her neck. 'I know.' Then he kissed her as if his life depended on it.

A few minutes later, feeling as if she were in the middle of a dream, Paige said, 'Though I have always liked men in suits.'

'Well, you can't have one. Not any more. I'm all you got now.'

She wrapped her arms around his neck and sighed. 'Fine. I think I can handle that.'

'All this? I guess we'll see.'

A flicker of something lit his eyes. Something dark and delicious. A warning, the boundaries of which she knew she was going to thoroughly enjoy pushing again and again and again if the heat that came along with it was anything to go by.

Her voice was husky as she said, 'You've spent the past day in airports or on planes so perhaps we could make a quick stop at home before we do any shopping.'

With a whoosh Gabe lifted her to standing and tucked the flamingos under one arm. 'I knew you were a woman after my own heart.'

Laughing, Paige went to press a button, then paused.

'Eighth floor,' Gabe said, tucking her beanie back onto her head. 'My place never felt like it was really mine. Yours, on the other hand, I like very much. Though it could do with a bigger TV. And I've seen inside your fridge and there's only so much celery and carrot and dip a real man can take. And that girly bed has to go—'

'Yeah yeah yeah,' Paige said, all the while knowing she wasn't letting him near the decorating aspect of her apartment. Except his bed. The thing was so glorious she'd carry that bed down from his apartment herself.

She pressed the emergency stop button, then the button for the eighth floor and leant her head on Gabe's shoulder as his arm wrapped around her waist. And waited for the lift to move. She'd waited her whole life for him, she could wait a few minutes longer.

This big brawny man who'd seen flamingos and thought of her. The dark, dangerous pirate who was prepared to buy a suit to marry her. The man who, when he went to Venice, or Brazil, or Timbuktu, would always be thinking about when he'd next be home.

A man who only had eyes for her.

EPILOGUE

———

Sam the Super leant back in his chair, shaking his head at the leggy blonde and the big guy from the top floor as they stared into one another's eyes like besotted teenagers on the lift's security monitor. They were both oblivious to the fact that he'd sent the lift to the penthouse and back to the lobby twice already.

She was hard work, the blonde, the way she couldn't just leave his little bit of fun with the lift well enough alone, but, he thought grudgingly, he admired her chutzpah. The other residents took his antics with the lifts for granted, but she never stopped trying to put things to rights. And while he was in a mood for admitting such things, he thought the new guy was all right too. He glanced at the box of cigars the guy had given him in thanks for helping him track down his bed.

Maybe he'd start to cut them a little slack. Maybe.

When the new guy reached up and cupped the blonde's chin, running his thumb over her cheek, Sam's mouth twitched in what felt like the beginnings of a warm smile.

When the black and white figures on the screen leant towards one another, clearly on the path to kissing, *again*, he mumbled beneath his breath, flicked off the monitor of the security camera. Sure, he liked to have his fun, a guy had to fill the hours of the day somehow, but they could keep their happily ever afters to themselves.

He pushed himself to standing with a groan and headed towards the service lift. It was time he changed the orange blossom mist in the foyer diffuser anyway.

* * * * *

REQUEST YOUR FREE BOOKS!
2 FREE NOVELS PLUS 2 FREE GIFTS!

H HARLEQUIN® KISS™

YES! Please send me 2 FREE Harlequin® Kiss novels and my 2 FREE gifts (gifts worth about $10). After receiving them, if I don't wish to receive any more books, I can return the shipping statement marked "cancel." If I don't cancel, I will receive 4 brand-new novels every month and be billed just $4.30 per book in the U.S. or $4.99 per book in Canada. That's a savings of at least 13% off the cover price! It's quite a bargain! Shipping and handling is just 50¢ per book in the U.S. and 75¢ per book in Canada.* I understand that accepting the 2 free books and gifts places me under no obligation to buy anything. I can always return a shipment and cancel at any time. Even if I never buy another book, the two free books and gifts are mine to keep forever.

145/345 HDN FVXQ

Name	(PLEASE PRINT)

Address	Apt. #

City	State/Prov.	Zip/Postal Code

Signature (if under 18, a parent or guardian must sign)

Mail to the Harlequin® Reader Service:
IN U.S.A.: P.O. Box 1867, Buffalo, NY 14240-1867
IN CANADA: P.O. Box 609, Fort Erie, Ontario L2A 5X3

Want to try two free books from another line?
Call 1-800-873-8635 or visit www.ReaderService.com.

* Terms and prices subject to change without notice. Prices do not include applicable taxes. Sales tax applicable in N.Y. Canadian residents will be charged applicable taxes. Offer not valid in Quebec. This offer is limited to one order per household. Not valid for current subscribers to Harlequin Kiss books. All orders subject to credit approval. Credit or debit balances in a customer's account(s) may be offset by any other outstanding balance owed by or to the customer. Please allow 4 to 6 weeks for delivery. Offer available while quantities last.

Your Privacy—The Harlequin® Reader Service is committed to protecting your privacy. Our Privacy Policy is available online at www.ReaderService.com or upon request from the Harlequin Reader Service.

We make a portion of our mailing list available to reputable third parties that offer products we believe may interest you. If you prefer that we not exchange your name with third parties, or if you wish to clarify or modify your communication preferences, please visit us at www.ReaderService.com/consumerschoice or write to us at Harlequin Reader Service Preference Service, P.O. Box 9062, Buffalo, NY 14269. Include your complete name and address.

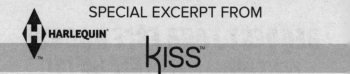
Nicky Sinclair is following doctor's orders, getting some well-needed rest and relaxation at her friend's family villa in Spain. But things take a twist when she finds her friend's sexy brother is there, too....

ONE MORE SLEEPLESS NIGHT

by Lucy King

"I was hurtling from time zone to time zone so much that I had no idea whether it was morning or night. Eventually I just wore out. Even taking my camera out of its case ended up becoming a major task, and that scared me witless because if I can't take photos I don't know what else there is." She ran a hand through her hair. "I think I just kind of gave up. I was so tired treading water, I simply stopped. And once I'd done that, then I really began to sink."

"That doesn't sound good," he muttered, knowing it was an understatement but too mystified by all the stuff beginning to churn around inside him to respond with anything more sensible.

"No, well, it wasn't," she said drily, "but it's why I ended up at your house. It's why when we met I was in a bit of a state. And it's why when you kissed me I couldn't respond, even though I desperately wanted to. When I told you that my lack of response to you wasn't you but me, I meant it. Along with everything else I'd lost all interest in sex. It was like I was dead inside."

"But not anymore."

She grinned. "Not anymore. And I've been taking pictures again. Of your vineyard. Do you mind?"

Did he mind? God, it was the least he could offer after all she'd been through. "Of course not."

What Nicky needed was looking after, Rafael decided darkly. She might act as if she was over what had happened, but was she? Really?

"So what plans do you have next?" he asked, ignoring the little voice inside his head demanding to know where he thought he was going with this, because she might not really be over it and she might need looking after but he definitely wasn't the sort of person who should be getting involved.

She lifted her eyebrows. "You mean beyond some more of that lovely restorative sex?"

"Beyond that."

She blinked and shrugged. "I don't know. I'm not very good at living beyond the present."

"Well, I'm at a loose end…. You're at a loose end…. What would you say to tying our loose ends together for a while?"

She grinned. "I'd say does that line really work?"

Rafael frowned, because oddly enough, it hadn't been a line. "I have no idea. You tell me."

**Pick up ONE MORE SLEEPLESS NIGHT
by Lucy King, on sale April 23 wherever Harlequin
books are sold.**

HARLEQUIN

KISS™

Use this coupon to
SAVE $1.00
on the purchase of
ANY 2
Harlequin KISS books.

Available wherever books are sold, including most
bookstores, supermarkets, drugstores and discount stores.

- ✂

SAVE $1.00 ON THE PURCHASE OF **ANY TWO** HARLEQUIN KISS BOOKS.

Coupon expires July 31, 2013. Redeemable at participating retail outlets
in the U.S. and Canada only. Limit one coupon per customer.

52610686

CANADIAN RETAILERS: Harlequin Enterprises Limited will pay the face value of this coupon plus 10.25¢ if submitted by customer for this product only. Any other use constitutes fraud. Coupon is nonassignable. Void if taxed, prohibited or restricted by law. Consumer must pay any government taxes. Void if copied. Nielsen Clearing House ("NCH") customers submit coupons and proof of sales to Harlequin Enterprises Limited, P.O. Box 3000, Saint John, NB E2L 4L3, Canada. Non-NCH retailer—for reimbursement submit coupons and proof of sales directly to Harlequin Enterprises Limited, Retail Marketing Department, 225 Duncan Mill Rd., Don Mills, ON M3B 3K9, Canada.

5 65373 00033 5   (8100)1 18300

U.S. RETAILERS:
Harlequin Enterprises Limited will pay the face value of this coupon plus 8¢ if submitted by customer for this product only. Any other use constitutes fraud. Coupon is nonassignable. Void if taxed, prohibited or restricted by law. Consumer must pay any government taxes. Void if copied. For reimbursement submit coupons and proof of sales directly to Harlequin Enterprises Limited, P.O. Box 880478, El Paso, TX 88588-0478, U.S.A. Cash value 1/100 cents.

HKCOUP0213A